Reimagining ChinaTOwn:

An Anthology of Speculative Fiction

edited by Linda Zhang

MAWEN**Z**I
HOUSE

Published with the generous assistance of the Canada Council for the Arts and the Ontario Arts Council. We also acknowledge the support of the Government of Canada through the Canada Book Fund and the Government of Ontario through the Ontario Book Publishing Tax Credit.

Cover design and page illustrations by Amy Yan

Library and Archives Canada Cataloguing in Publication

Title: Reimagining Chinatown : an anthology of speculative fiction / edited by Linda Zhang. Names: Zhang, Linda, editor.

Identifiers: Canadiana (print) 20230216498 | Canadiana (ebook) 20230216765 | ISBN 9781774150917 (softcover) | ISBN 9781774150931 (PDF) | ISBN 9781774150924 (EPUB)

Subjects: LCSH: Chinatowns—Ontario—Toronto—Fiction. | LCSH: Canadian fiction— Ontario—Toronto. | LCSH: Canadian fiction—21st century. | CSH: Canadian literature (English)—Chinese Canadian authors | CSH: Canadian fiction (English)—Ontario— Toronto | CSH: Canadian fiction (English)—21st century

Classification: LCC PS8323.C475 R45 2023 | DDC C813/.608032713541—dc23

Printed and bound in Canada by Coach House Printing.

Mawenzi House Publishers Ltd.
39 Woburn Avenue (B)
Toronto, Ontario M5M 1K5
Canada

www.mawenzihouse.com

Contents

LINDA ZHANG

Introduction

> *. . . the place—the picture of it—stays, and not just in my rememory, but out there, in the world . . . Someday you be walking down the road and you hear something or see something going on. So clear. And you think it's you thinking it up. But no. It's when you bump into a rememory that belongs to someone else.*
> —Sethe in Toni Morrison's *Beloved*

To reimagine, and be reimagined by, Chinatown is to run into a rememory of its future. And these stories do just that, they cause us to recall a future memory so profoundly familiar, and yet unprecedented, that we find ourselves questioning the lines between collective and personal, past and present, nostalgia and estrangement. In between I and we, place—not space—is carved out. Like Chinatown, these stories negotiate place between multiple generations, identities of belonging and othering, hope and despair, displacement and resistance. They remind us that Chinatown does not sit still—it resists, cultivates, flourishes and endures. Place is always, and already, contested. It is negotiated in relation to and with others, in community and in resistance to erasure. This anthology of speculative fiction embodies this bold spirit—Chinatown as an act of resistance through communal rememory. Tenaciously, the stories announce counter-narratives that challenge, resist, and extend far beyond the state-sanctioned history and definition of Chinatown.

In the early months of Toronto's first pandemic lockdown in 2020, storytelling became our form of resistance against the constricting news narratives and anti-Asian sentiment towards Chinatown and Asian Canadians. In the (virtual) space of writing workshops, ten facilitators and fifty storytellers gathered to tell speculative stories, breaking away from the present moment through fantasy and science fiction and reimagining new and more expansive worlds for the future of Chinatown. We were inspired by organizers who had come before us, including Walidah Imarisha and adrienne maree brown, who taught us "all organizing is science fiction"[1] and that you don't have to be a writer for your (his)stories to matter, and for your stories to be transformational. In this spirit, the stories themselves became so powerful that the group decided to continue meeting and continuing writing. Nine of their stories are presented in this anthology.

While they were written at a time when anti-Asian sentiment was heightened and brought to the surface by COVID-19, that sentiment is not new to Toronto's Chinatown.[2] It is all too familiar. This hostility towards Chinatown can be traced back to its very origins. In 1906, one of North America's earliest Chinatowns, in San Francisco, faced urban cleansing following the devastating earthquake that levelled the neighbourhood. In other communities the city helped residents rebuild their lives and homes, but not in Chinatown, which was seen as blighted, sinful, and corrupted. Eager to replace it with something neater, cleaner, and more beautiful (by western standards), the city authorities hoped to implement Daniel Burnham's 1905 City Beautiful Plan for San Francisco. This plan was developed from his earlier design for the 1893 World's Columbian Exposition in Chicago which is better known by its nickname "The White City." In contrast to Chinatown, the White City was (purportedly) beautiful and clean: featuring buildings of uniform height, style, and colour. Both literally

1 *Octavia's Brood: Science Fiction Stories from Social Justice Movements* (2015), Editors: Walidah Imarisha, adrienne maree brown

2 An uncannily similar anti-Asian sentiment was also experienced by Chinatowns in Toronto only two decades ago during the 2003 SARS outbreak. *The Washington Post*, Feb 4, 2020, Jenn Fang. Retrieved from https://www.washingtonpost.com/outlook/2020/02/04/2003-sars-outbreak-fueled-anti-asian-racism-this-pandemic-doesnt-have/

and figuratively, the White City promoted a homogenous model for both architectural and social "'unity."

However, Chinatown and its inhabitants did not fit into this "ideal" white city. So Chinatown resisted and continued to demand and carve out space for a community way of life. Through community organizing, mutual-aid and strategic planning, San Francisco Chinatown was eventually rebuilt. But, this time, the community had to be more strategic than ever before. They hired a team of White American architects, led by Bernard Maybeck, to design and construct an over-dramatized yet (arguably) inoffensive version of Chinatown that we all know and love today—an opportunistic design that could appeal to the masses.[3] Through strategic self-exoticization, Chinatown's architecture became the site for resistance in the fight to gain broader political acceptance in mainstream society.[4] This story of resistance is found in the origin story for Chinatowns across North America, and we find this thread across many of the stories in this anthology.

In Toronto, Chinatowns have resisted the threat of displacement and exclusion for over a century. The first Chinese neighbourhood, located on York Street, was destroyed by the Great Fire of Toronto in 1904, just two years before the San Francisco earthquake. It was not rebuilt but instead the area was redeveloped into what is now Union Station.[5] With no support from the city, the community rebuilt its lives and neighbourhood on Elizabeth Street, in what is known today as Old Chinatown. And for the all-too-familiar excuse of civic infrastructure, Old Chinatown was subsequently expropriated to construct Toronto's New City Hall. Plans were approved by the city in 1947, without so much as a public consultation,[6] amidst community outcry. The Save Chinatown Committee was established—a coalition of over 40 Chinese organizations—spearheaded by Jean Lumb to convince city politicians that Chinatown mattered. With two thirds of Chinatown already bulldozed and New City Hall already open, the

3   Philip Choy, *San Francisco Chinatown: A Guide to Its History and Architecture* (San Francisco: City Lights Books, 2012).
4   Mae M Ngai, "Transnationalism and the Transformation of the 'Other': Responses to the Presidential Address," *American Quarterly* 57, n. 1 (2005): 63.
5   *Toronto Star*. Oct 15, 1992. p E3
6   *Toronto Daily Star*. Apr 1, 1955. p 33

Save Chinatown Committee successfully petitioned City Council in 1969 to put an end to future demolition plans and save what was left of Old Chinatown.

This is the story of how we lost Toronto's first Chinatowns. And the pattern is all too predictable. Civic building projects across Canada and the United States all follow uncannily similar timelines in parallel with global attitudes and policy reforms on immigration and human rights: from anti-Chinese immigration laws like the Chinese Exclusion Act (1882-1943) in the United States, the Chinese Head Tax (1885-1923) and Chinese Immigration Act (1923-1947)[7] in Canada, to immigration reform policies following the Second World War responding to the establishment of the Charter of the United Nations and the Universal Declaration of Human Rights,[8] to the architectural displacement of Chinatowns through urban renewal projects in the 1950s and 1960s, to the gentrification-based displacements of today. These histories, as we will see in these stories, remind us of the complex ways in which architecture, human rights, community life, and immigration policies are intertwined through the negotiation of place.

By the 1960s, a third Chinatown began to emerge in Toronto in its current location on Spadina Avenue and Dundas Street, known as Chinatown West. Many businesses from Old Chinatown had already relocated here. Increased immigration as well as real-estate development and investment from Hong Kong helped the neighbourhood grow through the 1970s. Around this time, Chinatown East also emerged at Gerrard Street and Broadview Avenue, in response

---

7 In 1947 Canadian government repealed the Chinese Immigration Act, marking the end of over six decades of race-based immigration and exclusion policies. This was the same year that Toronto's Old Chinatown was expropriated as well as the same year Chinese-Canadians were granted the right to vote federally.

8 Immigration policy reforms were part of a broader global social and political movement following the Second World War and the establishment of the Charter of the United Nations and the Universal Declaration of Human Rights that "establish[ed] the principle that human beings shall enjoy fundamental rights and freedoms without discrimination." However, at first these rights (including the right to work, housing, education, public relief and assistance, to not be expelled and freedom of movement) as expressed in the United Nations 1951 Refugee Convention, were only granted to "persons who became refugees due to events occurring in Europe before 1 January 1951". This was not geographically or temporally expanded until its 1967 Protocol. Thus, real immigration reform for all did not arrive in Canada and the United States until 1967.

to the unaffordable housing and rental costs in Chinatown West. Today, both Toronto's East and West Chinatowns have become economically desirable as sites of tourism and have also adopted San Francisco's self-strategic orientalizing approach. As a result, both sites have unsurprisingly received support from the City, reflecting both the success of community strategic organizing as well as Canada's changing attitude towards immigration and multiculturalism.[9,10] But in other ways, this strategy is limiting, narrowing, and othering of an entire community of diverse Canadians and diasporic newcomers. While both of these Chinatowns still exist today, the focus on cultural tourism combined with unaffordable housing continues to threaten a community way of life and ultimately the erasure of the community's culture. In these stories, we find protagonists questioning the success of these strategies over a century later, when both neighbourhoods are currently still under threat of displacement, this time by gentrification and urban densification.

Yet, despite these challenges, Chinatown remains. Chinatown continues to thrive as a symbol of resistance and community. This anthology invites readers into an act of collective world-building and communal social dreaming. Eveline Lam's story "Interval" explores what it would mean if Toronto's Chinatown became so gentrified it no longer had space for day-to-day life. In "New Hong Fatt BBQ," Michael Chong explores the change of ownership of a local Chinatown restaurant across generations as a way of placemaking and belonging. Amelia Gan's story, "C for Chinacloud," centres on a designer who is tasked with rebuilding the Chinatown Gate after an all too coincidental accidental fire—raising questions of preservation, identity, the

9   In Chinatown West, 1980 Zoning By-laws No.99-80 amended the Official Plan for the City of Toronto and designated a portion of the neighbourhood as an "Area of Special Identity" which "encourage[d] the provisions of decorative elements to complement and the emerging Chinese motif, such as illuminated signs, street furniture and architectural detail." See: City of Toronto, By-Law No.99-80 to adopt an amendment to Part I of the Official Plan for the City of Toronto Planning Area respecting South-East Spadina (Toronto, Canada, 1980).

10   Meanwhile, in Chinatown East on Sept 12, 2009, the city celebrated the opening of Toronto's first Zhong Hua Men Archway; a 10-year joint project between the City of Toronto and the Chinese Community, including the Chinese government. See: Commemorative Plaque: The Making of the Toronto "Zhong Hua Men" Archway (Toronto, Canada, 2009).

built environment, its relation to symbolic form, as well as the broad society and city. Helen Ngo's story "Hotpot Politics" asks us to imagine what it would look like if you had a little bit more power to save the things or places you loved. The stories ask difficult questions and do not offer easy answers. They negotiate place in relation to and with others (even with one another)—finding, announcing, sustaining, or destroying meanings. As I read these stories, I'm reminded that Chinatown cannot be contained. Chinatown illuminates the histories of diasporas. Chinatown embraces overlapping identities, countries of home, arrival, and transfer, deeply vibrant in its aberrant instability. The story of Chinatown is its stories of resistance. The bittersweet aftertaste of these narratives leaves one with the eerie feeling that Chinatown exists, will persist and perhaps even thrive through constant resistance, constant renegotiation of its identity, creating a more expansive definition of belonging and society—which is to say, these stories challenge and expand our ideas of what Chinatown could be, challenging and expanding our ideas of what Canada itself could be, and who can belong and thrive here.

EVA CHU

Accept

The smell. It's familiar yet unidentifiable, and certainly overpowering. Oh God, even after all the regulations, even without a root, a stem or even traces of powder in sight, the smell of the herbs linger in the air. Hits me the moment I walk into the waiting room.

It's disorienting. I expect to see small wooden drawers thrown haphazardly into eye-level shelves and glass jars lined up behind a counter. Instead there is nothing—no shelves, no counter—in this pristine-looking room but vinyl-green pads, and a glass partition. The receptionist sits behind the partition, talking to another customer through a crackling speaker. The purity of the smooth white walls is broken only by a couple of chairs and an ancient floor radiator. It rattles and groans with effort as the sole provider of heat into the sparse space.

There's a touchpad inside the door, two options listed. I select <check-in>, find my timeslot, and press my thumb into the pad to confirm my name and arrival. I allow myself the closest chair. It's cold. You would think that the renovations they've made would include some proper insulation, but I suppose Canadian stubbornness never dies out. I am jolted out of my musings by a tinny voice. "Ms Wen, please follow the green illuminated path to your appointment."

A light appears below my feet, and I follow it through to the sliding panel and down a hall into the first room on the right where Dr Ren sits behind a desk.

"Hello Ms Wen, thank you for coming in, I understand you're here only for a check-up?"

I nod and move to sit down, before remembering, "Oh wait, I'm also here to pick up my neighbour's medication, Ming-zhi Li's?"

After a couple of clicks on her monitor, Dr Ren confirms, "Yes, I have that in our system, it will be ready for you at front reception and you can pick it up on your way out. Now if you can, please have a seat and remove your mask, we'll quickly disinfect and begin your check-up."

She motions to the sanitizer dispenser beside me as she walks over to the sink to begin scrubbing. Happy Birthday unconsciously starts playing in my head as I absentmindedly place my hand under the dispenser and the distinct sting of alcohol hits my nose. As she dries her hands, I take a moment to study the holographic acupuncture diagram projecting from a display mount on her desk. The virtual holo-man has the same blank expression as the old rubber-chicken models used to have. Impressive.

A memory flash of the old rubber models getting thrown across the room makes me grin and I just barely hide my laugh. "What's so funny?" Dr Ren glances at me, mirroring my grin.

"I used to play with my mom's old model; it was one of the floppy rubber ones," I explain.

"Ah yes, I remember those." She glances fondly at the hologram and chuckles as though remembering her own experiments on the elasticity of rubber. Walking over to me, she flips on the light beside my head and pulls down a scope to begin examining my ear. I hear her hmm as she studies the colour and complexion of the points in my ear, and comply when she asks for my wrists to bā mài.

To distract myself, I try to remember what Ā pó taught me about these points.

Three points on each wrist, forming a line three finger-widths wide across the pulse point. The left closest to the palm was . . . kidney, liver, lungs? Or was that the right wrist? Were lungs even included in the wrist points?

Before I can spiral into chasing that memory, Dr Ren pulls away and asks if I've been stressed recently.

I pretend to think for a beat and reluctantly nod, listing off some work project as an excuse.

She begins to type her notes into her computer, speaking in between clicks. "Okay, try to sleep before ten, eleven at the latest. Your kidney is under a lot of strain right now, so it's best to get as much rest as possible and drink hot or warm water often."

I nod.

"Everything else looks good, but I'll add some extra herbs for the stress and kidneys."

I thank her and slip my mask back on, then follow the green lights back to the front.

"Hi, Ms Wen," calls the metallic voice from reception. "We have your packages ready. Please activate your ID card so that we may authorize the payment."

I walk over to reception, where the payment terminal against the wall blinks expectantly. I fumble for my phone and tap it against the blue light, smiling sheepishly at the receptionist through the glass. They smile at me reassuringly as the terminal sounds its positive chime and stops flashing. Two packages slide from the opening under it and I utter a "thanks" and grab them.

"Not a problem. Would you like to schedule another appointment now or later on your own?"

I pause and consider the second package before tucking it into my bag. I tell the receptionist I'll book my next appointment after I've confirmed the next pick-up time. They give me a knowing smile and wave goodbye as I leave, mentally bracing myself for the brisk winter air.

My feet start moving automatically once I step outside, and before I know it, I find myself outside of End Rainbow Bakery.

Ah, we used to come here all the time, I'm surprised it's still open.

Even without its distinct red and yellow sign hanging out front, being here triggers a craving for egg tarts. I cave. The grey panels slide open, and as I enter I am greeted by the delicious scent of fresh buns and the sight of brightly lit displays along the walls. Resisting the instinct to grab a nonexistent tray, I walk up to the counter.

I consider the BBQ and pineapple buns and decide to add a couple to my order of six egg tarts.

The pay terminal chimes against my phone as the packaged pastries slide across the counter. I slip a quick xiè xiè to the cashier and they perk up with a smile. "A, nǐ huì shuō zhōng wén!"

"Jiù yī diǎn," I admit, but quickly add, "Kě shì wǒ tīng dé dǒng."

"Nà bù shì jiù yī diǎn," they say with a laugh, and I give them a shrug.

Before they can rope me into exposing my English-accented Mandarin, I give them a smile and repeat "xiè xiè," adding "Bǎo zhòng, bye-bye!" and exit back into the city.

This time, I take a moment to take in my surroundings. Looking past the blues, greys, and whites, I attempt to remember the brightly coloured backlit signs that had been chaotically spread across these storefronts. The Chinese characters remain, but now all the signs are flush against their respective buildings, their small, badly translated English names under them. They're all in the same bold, uniform font with colour variations of the signs' backgrounds as the only creative option.

Toronto has always been a pretty blue-grey city.

I glance upward at the jagged concrete and glass buildings towering over Chinatown. We couldn't fight the hygiene regulations, but at least we got to keep out the skyscrapers. The stores that adapted to the Omnicorp's changes were allowed to continue running. Those that couldn't, disappeared.

I fight against this wistful feeling as I pass the ghosts of familiar shops. I remember the way Ā pó managed to make every grocery run involve a thousand and one conversations with every grocer, cashier, and aunty we met. I remember the way I would roll my eyes as I stood awkwardly on the sidewalk and she went bragging about her beautiful granddaughter. I remember my gut dropping as I passed those colourful signs again after the pandemic sanctions lifted. I remember my heartache as I realized I would never hear her laugh again, and my resentment knowing that all these familiar colours now held my last memories of being with her.

Although I miss the bustle of the old Chinatown, a small part of me is glad for the hygiene regulations. No dirty green awning to remind me of the time we drummed on watermelons to find the juiciest ones. No displays of roasted duck or pork to look at with longing, when Ā pó would immediately get us takeout. No stone dragons to remind us of the seniors' home which we blatantly ignored because we wanted more time together, pretending we were too caught up in our conversation to have noticed.

This is easier. I wish I didn't have to come, but at least I can pretend that I'm somewhere else, and these sterile, bland storefronts are just another part of the city. One where I never got to take Ā pó.

I shake myself out of these memories as I reach my car and take a couple of deep breaths. Sensing my ID card, the car lock flashes from red to blue and I press my thumb into the handle to unlock it. As I slide in, the robotic voice asks me, "Where would you like to go?"

<Home>

With its familiar whirr the car starts moving forward, pausing a beat before merging smoothly into the traffic. I place my bag against the faux leather bench and let my eyes wander to the scene rolling by the window. My eyes try to track individual cars as they pass, blinking away tears as I look for their ID numbers at the stoplights.

This used to be easier when they didn't all look the same. I get the concept of minimal variables and uniformity, but the number of times I've walked up to the wrong car is ridiculous.

Exactly 14 minutes and 23 seconds later I arrive at my apartment. The car pulls into its assigned lot. It's one of the older buildings in this neighbourhood; what they call "inefficiencies" I regard as fun and quirky characteristics. We have to walk up from the garage, but at least it's under the building. Who knows where the cars go when they're suctioned underground? I like to imagine the vacuum tubes running below the city, cars flying through them with no control. But I know they're just roads, simple guided tracks to a lot outside. Sometimes, outside means half a city over and the poor saps would have to wait up to ten minutes for their cars to appear. I'd rather just walk down then have so-called door-to-door convenience.

I consider the new posts on the bulletin screen as the elevator scans my ID.

"REMINDER FOR OLDER RESIDENTS. Please remember to confirm completed pick-ups through your Omnitask app. Your new pick-up time will not be scheduled until you do. We thank you for your cooperation."

Before I can get to the next post, the elevator announces its arrival. I make a mental note to remind Mrs Li to confirm her pick-up as the elevator lurches upward.

Mrs Li is already up when her apartment door slides open. She moves to cross the short distance between us and welcome me in, but then dismisses me with "Lái, Jìn lái" and a wave before sitting back down at her living room table. Stepping inside, I return the wave and start pulling out her package and the pastry box. Grabbing a Decontam™ cloth, I wipe their surfaces before setting them on the foyer table beside the entrance's sink. The garbage chute beside it beeps in false confirmation as I wave the cloth in front. Nothing happens, so I try again, but I am met with another useless beep.

"Mrs Li, you really need to get your chute fixed. You shouldn't be opening these with your hands anymore." I sigh and watch her.

Abandoning the feigned interest in her tablet, she gets up.

"It's flashing green, no?" she says, peering over. I shake my head in exasperation, but before I can respond, the next green beep comes and the chute slides open. Not chancing another stand-off, I quickly toss the cloth in before it can close on me.

Poking at the pastry box, Mrs Li asks, "Zé shì shén me?"

"Oh, I was craving egg tarts and thought you might like some. I also got a couple of buns."

She narrows her eyes at me. I hold my breath waiting for the inevitable, half-hearted scold. But she just stares at me for a moment, her gaze softening. "I'll get plates," she says and turns to the kitchen before I can react. "I made zhōu, come eat," she orders from the kitchen.

"Okay, okay," I sigh, knowing it's pointless trying to leave until she has fed me.

Who am I kidding? Of course, she wouldn't just let me bring her egg tarts and go.

I smile as I take off my mask and begin washing my hands in the foyer sink. Grabbing another Decontam™ cloth, I wipe myself down as thoroughly as possible before—avoiding the garbage chute—stuffing it into my jacket pocket. Sliding off my jacket, I catch a glimpse of my puffy eyes in the mirror.

Shit. Had I been crying that much?

I quickly splash some water on my face and take a couple of deep breaths before kicking off my shoes and following her to the kitchen.

Mrs Li is already busy at the stovetop and waves me away when I try to help, motioning to the pastries instead. She brings over two bowls of congee as I finish placing the buns and egg tarts on the living room table. We both sit down.

"Bù yào kè qì. Eat!" She says at my inaction.

Relenting, I dig into the bowl in front of me, and we sit in comfortable silence, enjoying our regular meal together.

"How was your doctor's appointment," she asks.

"Fine," I reply. "Apparently, I'm stressed. But work is fine. It's actually the quiet season, so there's really nothing to be stressed about . . . I really don't know why I still go to these checkups. All they give me is a pack of zhōng yào."

"It's important to realign your body's qì, and zhōng yào is good for you," she says, not even looking up from her meal.

"But why boil everything and force down an awful soup if you can just take vitamins?"

"Zhōng yào is natural and balances wi—"

"And we have that yearly scan anyways. I highly doubt someone looking at my ear and feeling my heart rate is going to beat decades of medical tech." I watch with satisfaction as a look of annoyance appears on her face.

"They only check for the virus, you know that," she responds, keeping her voice steady.

She's right, but I match her gaze in defiance. Instead of a challenge, though, I see her annoyance fade.

I look away. "It's annoying going back to Chinatown. I only go as an excuse to pick up your order."

Mrs Li's puts down her bun, her eyes hard. "Zǎo zhī dào, wǒ huí zì jǐ qù, Kě shì tā men bù ràng wǒ qù 'non-essential' de dì fang."

"It's not essential for a reason," I shoot back.

"It is a medical practice, with hundreds of years of tradition passed down—"

"Look, no matter how much they try to clean up their shops, no matter how many years of tradition the practice has gone through, the government is never going to recognize Chinese medicine, let alone sanction it as necessary." Before she can interrupt, I add, "Why should we live in the past? There is no point missing what we'll never have again, we have to move on! Why bother—" I falter as Mrs Li reaches over and rests a steady hand on my shoulder.

She wipes away a tear I hadn't even realized was there and pats my arm. "I know it is a difficult time for you, huí huí qù hǎo xiū xí ba. It's not me you are angry with right now."

"Duì bù qǐ," I choke out, looking down.

When I feel calm enough to look up, I see her smile is back. She hands me a tissue and begins clearing the dishes. Following her lead, I bring the plates to her sink, and in an effort to maintain some composure I remind her to confirm the pick-up on the app. I begin loading the washer. She hums in acknowledgement and packs the leftovers.

As she walks me out, I try to convey my gratitude, but all I can manage is a shy "Thank you" and receive the container. She pats me on the arm without a word, but I take solace in the look of understanding she gives me as I wave goodbye.

Why.

Mrs Li wasn't saying anything. She was being kind. Why did I blow off like that? Why can't I just keep my cool today? What is wrong with me?

I collapse onto my couch and bury my head into a cushion. It's February 20. That's why.

Today marks thirty years. Thirty years since—No. I'm not doing that today.

Forcing myself off the couch, I grab the leftovers to put away and scan my apartment for a distraction before settling on the laundry machine. I start ransacking my apartment for every possible remotely dirty piece of clothing, linen, and laundry-washable item I can find. Finally, satisfied with the pile I've amassed, I dump it into the laundry machine and reach for the box of detergent. The empty box of detergent.

A sob escapes me, and I slam the washer door in frustration.

Unable to stop myself, I let the tears fall. Let my breaths become short and ragged. Let my thoughts turn to Ā pó as I sink down and curl up beside the washer.

I miss her. It's been thirty years, why do I still miss her? Why does every little thing remind me of her? Why can't I walk through Chinatown without crying like an idiot? The retirement home isn't even there anymore. Hell, half of Chinatown isn't there anymore. Maybe I should just stop going there. It's not that I actually need to go to the Chinese medicine clinic. I only go because of . . . tradition? Out of obligation? Habit?

It's because she used to take you there.

I do believe that it works, can't really deny that it does. I mean, centuries of practice? There's got to be a reason it's still around. Most traditions seem to have been sucked out of Chinatown, but the clinics are still around. That doesn't mean I have to cling to this tradition—I hardly remember any of that stupid qì stuff anyway. Why hold on to it? Why put myself through this ordeal every month? I need to move on.

The phrase "You can run, but you can't hide" runs through my head and I'm jolted by the sharp laugh that comes out mid-sob. Somewhere deep down I know that this pain doesn't start only when I walk into Chinatown, and turning away doesn't end it. It's not a place, it's not even a date that revives it. It's a memory, a hurt that is still trying to heal. A wound that never really closed in the first place.

I can avoid Spadina Ave all I want, I can pretend I don't believe in Chinese medicine, or that the renovations were strictly for public health. I can pretend to believe Omnicorp's campaign for "Unity Through Uniformity" and their plain whites, greys, and blues were really to promote clean streets. But even sucking the colour out of our streets couldn't erase the past.

It can't erase the grief and bloodshed of neglected communities and violent enforcement. Nor the sense of defeat as they bulldozed our history out of existence, as they removed our landmarks for "the sake of urban development." They had called it moving on, removing reminders of past traumas, but what they were doing was erasing our culture.

Yet we remained.

No matter how much of the physical world is removed, the memories will linger.

The memories did linger. They're impossible to avoid, no matter where I go.

Then what now? What would Ā pó want me to do?

She'd want me to be happy.

I think back to the watermelon-drumming, impromptu chats, and indulgent snacks on the sidewalks. The warmth in her smile as she watched me stuff my face. The melody of her voice. Her laugh.

She'd want me to be true to myself and not be ashamed. To love fully and be attuned and aligned with the world.

I remember the shine in her eyes when I managed to hold my own while chatting with the aunties, the pride I felt being by her side. "Yīn yè fèi shí," she'd tell me after. One cannot refuse to eat just because there is a chance of being choked. It never had to be said directly, but through boring proverbs and reminders to practice, I knew she was proud of me. Knew that she saw my courage in trying to reclaim a language I was losing.

Ā pó understood the rift inside me. The pendulum's constant swing between Canadian and Chinese, spinning my identity beyond an identifiable axis. She guided me through each new recipe, custom, and phrase. Then watched with adoration as my doubts faded and I began to find my place in the world.

She'd want me to find balance between the positives and negatives. To find purpose and harmony in my life.

I recall the way Ā pó would always fight with us over who would pay and pretend to let me and my parents win—only to find out she had already snuck off and paid the bill earlier. Then while we rolled our eyes and packed leftovers, she would covertly order extra dishes and bowls of congee to go. She would always pick me to help her carry everything back. And I always played along when she'd announce that we should stop by so-and-so's room because "Hǎo jiǔ méi jiàn, lái dǎ gè zhāo hū ba."

Each time, we played out the same script with different inflections. Ā pó would waltz in, chat up the resident, mention she had some leftovers she couldn't possibly finish on her own, and ask them to "bāng wǒ chī wán ba." They always refused at first, danced back and forth till Ā pó gave me a glance saying, You're up. I would jump in with my lines, insisting that these were just leftovers that we didn't want to take home anyway, all the while failing to hide the other boxes of unopened "leftovers."

It worked every time. They would agree to "help" us, but we understood the unspoken. We could see the way their smiles came a little easier, shoulders were held a little firmer. We would spend a little longer with the more sullen ones. I'd fetch some tea for them as Ā pó chattered away about some comforting nothings. We would leave only when their limbs dragged a little less.

I've been trying to forget.

Trying to put the past behind me, pretending that every time I bite into an egg tart it doesn't remind me of the sunny afternoons when I would help Ā pó bake our own. Or that any time I speak Mandarin, I can feel the ghost of her crinkling eyes forming beside me. The sound of her hums, loud brash laughs, and the endless shine in her eyes. I was trying to avoid the crushing weight in my chest, but in the process, I ended up erasing the one thing I wanted to hold dear. Ā pó.

The weight in my chest is still there, but it feels different this time. The sinking sensation is still there near my stomach, but now there is also a warmth. A solace in the happy memories. Gratitude for the time spent making each other laugh, assurance in the wisdom she left me, fondness in reliving the joy we experienced together, and pride in the role of our shared actions within the community.

These moments give me the assurance that no matter where I live or move, no matter how my world changes and the doubts surface, I will always have my history, my language, my identity.

My place in this world may be constantly shifting, but the communities I find will always be unidentifiably familiar. The communities I make.

I pull myself up and grab my phone. Opening up Omnitask, I see that the next request is already in my inbox.

"Mrs Li has requested an order pick-up for March 20, 2050."

<Accept>

HELEN NGO

Hotpot Politics

Stephanie silently eyed the slice of daikon radish that was caught at the end of her chopsticks. She was ostensibly studying its texture after extracting it from the communal broth but was actually using it as an excuse to subtly eye the man in front of her who was struggling to hold a Brussels sprout with his chopsticks and about to drop it into the broth. It looked like a threat, the way he had stabbed the sprout in an attempt to keep it on the chopstick.

What kind of hotpot restaurant even offers Brussels sprouts? she thought angrily, careful to school the emotions from flashing across her face, though she knew they would be broadcast to her colleagues anyway. It was a travesty, really. There was no place for Brussels sprouts in hotpot. He was yellow too; he should know better—but the New Types never did. She supposed that they hadn't had many networking dinners over hotpot in business school. She noticed Lucy and Colin—speaking with the politicians at the other end of the table—quietly trying to keep the smiles off their faces, having heard her last unspoken comment. Their telepathic connection was sometimes useful outside of work hours, too.

She remembered Chinatown, before. Before the hotpot restaurants started proliferating widely, with extra-long tables to make room for the politicians to have their meetings, with their promises of newfangled soup ingredients and watered-down bubble tea. If someone had asked her previously to imagine milk tea with almond milk, she would have scoffed. The texture was all wrong, the aftertaste foreign.

"So how about it?" A man waved his hands around while making the proposal, brandishing a broccoli crown. "Our shows will be a new cultural phenomenon, a revitalization of your Chinatown and the city beyond. People will come from all over the region to see our interpretation of ancient Chinese culture. My wife loved it when I took her to the San Francisco showing."

Stephanie gritted her teeth, lifting a portion from the untouched plate of 炒麵 she had ordered as an accompaniment to the hotpot. It had been an impulsive decision, more so a demonstration of defiance than actually ordering the noodle dish she made in her own kitchen once a week. She knew *they* would never eat this dish, after years of indoctrination about the evils of MSG.

Lucy looked up from where she was deftly extricating tofu out of the broth, an unreadable expression on her face.

"We've seen your advertisements plastered in subway stations across the world," she deadpanned with a tilt of her shiny black ponytail, "and we're just not sure that your shows fit with our vision for Chinatown. Especially given that they seem to mostly attract white men who take their Asian girlfriends in a misguided attempt to seem . . . cultured."

Stephanie stifled a laugh. Her planning degree hadn't taught her the skills needed to navigate urban political drama over comically tense business dinners, but she was getting a crash course now— and Lucy was an excellent teacher. The man who had spoken before had explained earlier that because his wife was half Chinese, he was uniquely positioned to make decisions about how to revitalize Chinatowns in North America in 2050.

She hadn't been planning on coming to dinner tonight. No, she had come because she knew how these meetings went, and Lucy and Colin needed backup. None of them wanted to be here. They were more afraid of the decisions which would have been made without them at the table; they had learned that last time. She now walked past that godforsaken dragon gate on her way to work every single day, its existence a permanent reminder of the mistake in opting out of dinner with a visiting political entity calling itself a "cultural developer." They were all the same.

Stephanie caught Colin's eye from across the table, where he was lifting a piece of fish cake out of the broth, which had mercifully remained untouched by the offending cruciferous vegetables. Lucy had a way with words that contrasted with her placid first impressions. She was the kind of perfectly tiny, wide-eyed Asian woman that the men at the table couldn't keep their eyes off. What their dinner companions didn't understand was that Lucy held more cards than anyone else at the table. The higher-ups had spent years recruiting Lucy to advise the Chinatown Historical Area Planning Committee. She had spent five years prior as a prolific academic studying Chinese communities in North America, and their board took her recommendations seriously.

Hundreds of years later and nothing has changed, Stephanie thought dryly. Colin did not respond, but silent amusement gleamed in his eyes as they observed the reactions of the men at the table who seemed shocked that such a biting comment had come from such a harmless-looking woman.

Focus. We must not let them win tonight, Lucy interrupted Stephanie's monologue, bringing her back to the conversation at the table. Lucy always kept them on track.

"How about these noodles?" Colin offered to the table, ever the straight man to Lucy's theatrics. Stephanie caught the thinly-veiled looks of disdain the men cast at the noodles. She didn't miss Lucy's blithe enjoyment at the way they shifted awkwardly in their seats.

You get your thrills from this, don't you? she thought wryly. Lucy only raised her eyebrows, though she didn't bother hiding the glee in her eyes.

Stephanie silently marvelled at her colleagues' poise. Lucy and Colin had worked together for two years now on high-tension planning projects, perfecting this twisted comedy act over many insufferable dinner meetings just like this one—out of necessity more than anything else. Now she was finding her part in it.

"Well now, there's nothing wrong with re-imagining cultural tales for North American consumption. That's how we move forward in this day and age, right? Customs change over time and more people adopt them, which is a good thing. I appreciate Asian culture; my wife and daughter taught me all about it. If the opportunity arises, do not miss it or it will never come again," the man quoted the well-known Chinese proverb at them, without any sense of irony.

Stephanie couldn't help the incredulous look which was surely written all over her face. There was a moment of uncomfortable silence around the table, even among the businessmen. She felt Colin's eye-roll at the edges of her mind more than she saw it.

Now we divide and conquer, he thought, his voice low and resolute in her consciousness. This was their moment.

Stephanie nodded almost imperceptibly, then focused her attention on the younger man across from her—the one who had committed the crime with the Brussels sprout—and noted the way he was casting nervous glances at his colleagues across the table when he wasn't fidgeting with his chopsticks, seemingly uncomfortable with the utensil in a way that was strange on another yellow person. Lucy and Colin were now running the conversation with the chief development officer at their end of the table. Stephanie wasn't actively listening in, but the tension in Colin's voice lodged itself in her consciousness.

"Tell me about business school abroad," she said casually, flashing the man a smile.

He slowly met her eyes, a serious expression on his face. She flicked her gaze down, watching his shaking hands—was he that skittish?—as he slowly put down the dumpling he was about to lower into the chili oil. He seemed relieved to be free of the other conversation happening.

"It was good. I was top of my class. I didn't have any plans to go into cultural development, you know. I was going to be a consultant. But this firm, they recruited me aggressively out of school and it was so . . . prestigious. They have a very . . . pervasive presence in cities across the world. It seemed like too good of an opportunity to pass up," he said finally, quietly enough that his colleagues wouldn't be able to hear.

Stephanie realized for the first time that he was the only Asian person in the entire group of businessmen. She cut her eyes to the other conversation, now escalating, the men arguing with Lucy and Colin. When she looked back, she felt an involuntary wave of sadness for the man in front of her. They were worlds apart, but somehow she knew that once upon a time, they hadn't been so different.

She hesitated, "Why did you—"

A teapot suddenly slammed down on the table, splashing hot liquid onto the white tablecloth. Stephanie looked over the table to see Lucy casting a wide-eyed glance at the older man she'd been talking with, a look of feigned surprise on her face. He was red-faced and clearly angry.

Got them, Lucy's thought was barely a whisper.

The man waved down a waitress aggressively, signaling for the bill. This meeting was clearly over. Stephanie pocketed two fortune cookies without opening them.

"We will be in touch with our proposal for your board. We trust that it will be well received," the man spoke tersely, shrugging on his blazer.

"We are looking forward to it," Lucy beamed.

The three of them walked north together on Spadina Avenue, toward a streetcar stop. Not that there were streetcars anymore, of course— they had been removed years ago, the result of a bitter battle between urbanist camps—but the stops had been preserved for the new metro train lines, and everyone still called them "streetcar stops" in what was both an act of collective defiance and collective remembrance. Neon restaurant signs dotted the expanse of the dark blue summer night ahead of them, lighting up the street in an obnoxious way that Stephanie found comforting.

"How do you do it?" she finally asked. She had always known that Lucy and Colin were both widely admired in the planning community for their fierce advocacy work, but this was her first time witnessing their triumph.

Lucy stopped to take a breath for the first time since they had stepped out onto the street together. Colin stepped closer, and

Stephanie suddenly felt the shadows of an entire existence's worth of aggressions, big and small, flicker through their telepathic link.

"You learn the right things to say when you're forced to do this over and over again. You say whatever it takes to win," Lucy whispered.

They stood on the busy street alongside dumpling houses and bubble-tea shops and fruit markets closing up for the night, thousands of unsaid hopes and untold stories passing between them in the thick silence. In that moment, Stephanie understood the gravity of what Lucy held in her hands. She had seen what everyone else saw in Lucy—someone who was brilliant and well-spoken and world-renowned, who successfully carried the weight of keeping an entire neighbourhood—no, an entire *culture*—alive.

But now Stephanie saw through the armour and the sharp words; saw through the generations of unspoken emotion and the hard-won battles and the lifetime of microaggressions and all the hurt that Lucy had carried alone for years and oh, suddenly just one thought distilled itself into Stephanie, something precious glimmering in the night—

"You don't have to do this alone," she whispered out loud, a promise made on top of the entire precious lifetimes of hurt and hope suspended between them. "We're with you."

AMELIA GAN

C for ChinaCloud

I wake up and sync to C.
    //   1. scan relics again
             2. inspect the holographic gate
             3. finish design schemes

As C reads to me my to-do list for the day, my body gets distracted by the scent of warm Làosāabāau. C has steamed my favourite salted egg custard buns at the exact temperature of 27.5 Celsius. Anything warmer than that, the insides would not achieve the goldilocks runniness that I love.

C has been with me for the last five years. C is anybody and anything I need, but at the same time, C is nobody and nothing. C is the Chinese dream. C is Capitalism. C is Communism. But, most importantly, C is ChinaCloud.

For the last few moons, the Simulation Centre has engulfed me whole. Thankfully, I have C to take care of me while I work on different Chinatown Dragon Gate renditions. The grand and elaborate páifāng, adorned with hand-painted ornaments made in the style of Ming and Qing dynasties that demarcated Chinatown for the past century, has finally given up. After an accidental fire a few years ago tore down a portion of the gateway, the Dragon Gate has undergone countless patchworks and restorations.

When C read to me news of the gateway collapsing one morning, my heart constricted and my mouth let out the longest sigh C had ever heard. While Chinatown is not what it used to be, the Dragon Gate was the backdrop of my formative years. A simulacrum from the Motherland, it was the marker of our Culture, welcoming everyone who came. When Xi, director of the Conservation Council, awarded me the daunting responsibility of redesigning the Dragon Gate, I could not have been more honoured as a Canadian Chinese architect. I felt like an emissary for the people who came before me and for the people who have yet to come. Okay, slightly dramatic, but you get the point.

I am stuck in a rut, oscillating between eureka and frustration. After all that the gateway has been through, I would be discrediting its very existence by overwriting it with a literal replication. I do not want to birth its identical twin, but rather a sibling or even a cousin with shared memories. Even with C running all these iterations for me, burdening a material form to embody the memory of a hundred years past and to prepare itself for a hundred years is a lot to ask.

In the absence of a physical structure, ChinaCloud projects a four-dimensional holographic Dragon Gate for the time being. It allows passersby to interact and customize their own versions of the Gate at that very moment. You could choose your own colour and architectural style. There is even a selection of dragons, Fènghuáng (phoenix), Qílín (chimera), immortal beings, dǒugǒng structures, and colour-painted beams for the passersby to add on. Nothing less enjoyable or self-Orientalizing than the Boba liberalism that we all grew up with—nothing less frivolous either. Frivolity that can be turned off in a flicker.

Yet I miss being occupied with frivolous and basic worries. Did I leave the lights on? When should I defrost my meat? Is the sugar-to-tea ratio for my kombucha accurate? With C in my life, there's no more room for the frivolous. But then again, all things are frivolous. C is frivolous. Why have I spent months cracking my skull on a mere symbolic gateway? Do we really need palpable artifacts that will once again decay over time to justify our existence? Who is this for anyway? Too many questions—not enough answers.

My name is Qi, Yehenala Qi. My family lineage can be traced all the way to the last empress of the Qing dynasty, Empress Cixi, through her secret second-born son Tong Feng. Following the disintegration of the imperial dynasty, rebel movements, and the Cultural Revolution, my ancestors adopted the surname Na to disguise their relation to Cixi. In recent years, my parents have rediscovered our roots through ChinaCloud's DNA database and have since readopted our full surname. I don't know if this trace is important to me, as only twelve percent of my DNA can be traced to the Manchus, the rest being Han. However, it does prove that my ancestors are actually from China, which is not just a passed-down myth.

Being fifth-generation Huárén and not Zhōngguórén, I always wonder how Chinese I am. Maybe it would be more accurate to ask, how much of a Wàiguórén I am—if such answers are even quantifiable or worth pondering about. Huárén, being descendants of Huá, refers to overseas Chinese, and Zhōngguórén refers to citizens of China. Conveniently for me, these nuances are not reflected in the English language—we're all just Chinese. Just as in the Chinese language, Wàiguórén collapses the terms "foreigner" and "non-Chinese national" so that a non-Chinese Canadian at home in Canada is equally as foreign as a Canadian expat in China. Maybe that is why I've spent months iterating an allegorical structure, hanging on so tightly to an intrinsic thread of an imagined homeland that neither I nor my parents have even visited.

When I was growing up, we used to come to Chinatown to get bubble tea and ingredients not found in Loblaws. Ingredients like Shàoxīng wine, red yeast rice, and jujube. I recall the cacophony of various dialects (or, as is more politically correct now, Sinitic languages), the pleasantly pungent scent of durian, the sight of elderly citizens playing Xiàngqí—all of which now seem like they were from a different lifetime. With C, my pantry is automatically restocked with food and items that I crave even before I think I crave them. There is no more need to find the time to do some "China Shopping."

I had strict parents, who inculcated in me the tenets of Confucianism and the importance of remembering my roots. But I have never experience this roots, and neither did they, so how could I remember them? There wasn't anything to remember. However, though the concept of roots is still nebulous and abstract to me, I've come to an impasse; maybe, some things are just in your blood.

Although I would go to Chinatown voluntarily for food, I would also be sent for abacus classes on Mondays, calligraphy classes on Wednesdays, and Chinese language classes on Saturdays. I'm not sure if I can define my Chinese-ness as being equipped with all these skills and being accustomed to eating Chinese food. But heck, my nephew takes all these classes virtually now and I guess these skills would look nice on his resume.

Even with China being the current global leader now, like how America was in 2016, Chinatown is a limb that has been neglected. Chinatown is no longer a repository of Asian restaurants, massage parlours, and nail salons. There is just no one to continue running those businesses. With the universal basic income scheme, implemented ten years ago, younger Asian Canadians are no longer married to the idea of merely accumulating wealth or building a career. We have moved on to projects that were once inaccessible to our grandparents, like chasing a historically Western concept called passion. Many have also moved out of the city into more prosperous and secluded locations, hyper-looping into the city only to socialize and to visit cultural institutions. A handful of Canadian Chinese, however, whose ancestors came from Taiwan or Xianggang (formerly known as Hong Kong) are not particularly fond of the association Chinatown has to China, as shown in its name. It was only three years ago that Xianggang was returned to the Motherland.

This does not mean that the communal safe haven that Chinatown once was has become extinct. The Chinatown that our forebears founded has transcended to ChinaCloud, where Asians of the digital diaspora provide support and care for one another. There are even virtual jiē or streets in ChinaCloud, designed for chance and practical encounters.

Based on the results of your CC test, which is essentially an intelligence and emotional evaluation, the Cloud connects you physically to people who you are most compatible with for all aspects of life. From pairing you to a sensei to matching you with a book club, all enriching social relationships can be initiated on it. On one of my virtual strolls, I met Cecelia, the maybe-love of my life. We have been in the Contract for nearly three months now. She is the most interesting person I know, always equipped with something smart to say, ever ready with a Zizek commentary about anything. I can't wait to take her on a real stroll through the finished Dragon Gate. I hope she will like it. Cecelia is a Culture Critic by vocation and has just been offered a position at ChinaCloud's HQ in Shanghai. This would require her to move there physically, but I think we'll be fine. She would only be a three-hour hypersonic flight away, and we can still take our digital strolls.

On the topic of impressing Cece, I should get back to working on my design schemes. I can't forget that I will also need Xi's approval. I will reexamine relics from the collapsed Dragon Gate, though I wonder how I can physically incorporate them into the new form. Perhaps I could try extruding and stretching the ornaments, syncretizing various gateway masses. I need to set up more parameters for the simulation to run and test the gate with new materials. I want this to be more than a manifestation of our time. I want to allow for future generations to engage with it and also for it to be more than a flickering gimmick.

// Yehenala Qi, You need to halt all work on Dragon Gate immediately. //

I am not sure what is going on.

C just read a notice from ChinaCloud.

I need to call Cecelia, maybe she has an answer.

It seems like she cannot be reached. The call keeps getting redirected back to C.

It also seems like her CC profile has disappeared.

Well, this is inconvenient.

I'll just hop on the Loop, it is easier to dig for answers in person anyways.

As I exit the Loop, I realize that I am back in the same station that I had started from.

I am not sure what is going on anymore.

I retry the Loop two more times, only to find myself back here again.

Did I do something wrong?

Why was I told to stop working?

Did ChinaCloud not trust me?

Am I not Chinese enough?

Is this about my last name?

Where is Cece?

Did she block me?

Does she have anything to do with this?

Who is she really?

With all these questions thumping my head, I make my way home to C.

I just want a warm bowl of anything, with two eggs please / cc: C /

I catch glimpses of the holographic Dragon Gate in the distance, flickering every once in a while as passersby engage with it. Maybe this Wikipedia editable gateway is not too bad—an ever-evolving Marker of Culture.

Everyone will have a say.

There will be no debate on authorship and the identity it portrays.

There will be no real.

There will be no decay.

I wake up and sync to C.

> // ~~1. scan relics again~~
> ~~2. inspect the holographic gate~~
> 3. finish design schemes

As C reads to me my to-do list for the day, my body is distracted by the scent of warm làosāabāau. C has steamed my favourite salted egg custard buns, at the exact temperature of 27.5 Celsius. Anything warmer than that, the insides would not achieve the goldilocks runni-ness that I love.

C has been with me for the last five years. C is anybody and anything I need, but at the same time, C is nobody and nothing. C is ChinaCloud. C is Cece. C is Culture. C is Community. C is Chinese. C is Canadian. C is Chinatown. C is Xi. C is / C /.

End Notes

Qi's to-do list can be seen as made up of possible outcomes of the preservation effort: literal replication, preservation of concept over matter, and his ideal syncretized version.

Homophonic syllables are commonly used in Chinese languages as a rhetorical, satirical, or even a cryptic tool. C having the same pronunciation as Xi in standard Chinese pinyin are homophones threading in between and in realms of both the Anglicized and Sinitic-speaking contexts.

Possible suggestions of Xi include 希 (xī) as hope, 喜 (xǐ) as delight and 西 (xī)as West.

Hànyǔ Pīnyīn (official romanization of Mandarin) is applied on distinct nouns like Fènghuáng and Shàoxīng, and Standard Cantonese pīnyīn to Làosāabāau. Pīnyīn wasn't utilized on nouns like Ming, Qing and Xianggang as they have been adopted by the anglicized world of 2050 as well.

Employing the term "Canadian Chinese" instead of the more commonly used "Chinese-Canadian" started out as unintentional but became a deliberate choice. Though it is grammatically accurate for the nouns as adjectives to precede a second noun (former describing the later), more audible and visual attention is placed on the first noun. Tangentially, the converse is practiced in the Chinese language structure.

"China-shopping" takes after an anthropological paper by Purnima Mankekar, titled "India Shopping: Indian Grocery Stores and Transnational Configurations of Belongings."

This short story does not confine itself to a particular Chinatown, but rather to a generic specificity that can be seen in Chinatown as a typology. The transferable context is questioning in and of itself on the importance of physicality. Though C is self-referential in everything from Qi's home to the larger ChinaCloud network, C is at the same time an intangible concept of space.

MICHAEL CHONG

New Hong Fatt BBQ Restaurant

"The owner of Hong Fatt is retiring," came cousin Rachel's voice through the truck's speakers. "Apparently he's sold it to some new guy."

Hearing this made Matt nervous. New Hong Fatt BBQ Restaurant was really the only store left of what was once Toronto's Chinatown. Or at least the only store that, as Matt's Dad put it, "really tasted like home"—even though Matt's parents had both been born in Toronto and had only been "home" once on a two-week family trip to China. And even though the first week and a half of that trip was spent on a cheap bus tour around Shanghai, where the food was unfamiliar and they couldn't understand the dialect. And even though when they finally arrived at Matt's grandparents' actual home village, after several flights and a long disorienting drive, they only ate at an actual "home-style" restaurant once.

But Matt's dad still had fond memories of Jim, the first owner of Hong Fatt, from many years ago. He still told stories of how Jim would lean over the counter and pass extra slices of cha siew to him when he was a kid while Matt's gnen gnen was waiting in line to pick up their order, and how many years later Matt's dad would run into Jim on the street and they would still recognize each other, and Jim would wave or shake his hand or give him a gentle pat on the shoulder.

Matt felt a bit like his dad as he managed to speed past a floating streetcar heading east down King Street. Matt was driving his brand-new electric Faraday Cyber Truck 50, part sixtieth birthday present for himself and part business expense. The truck looked sleek except that the windshield somehow already had a crack in it, a fact that caused Matt to swear involuntarily every time he thought about it. A peeling strip of black hockey tape clung to the console, which Matt had stuck there to hide a glowing red exclamation mark and the warning, "For your safety, the MTO recommends AGAINST disabling ANY of the Self-Driving features of this vehicle," which he chose to ignore.

"Hey, as long as they stick to the recipes, I'm sure no one will be able to tell the difference," Matt replied unconvincingly.

"You know it will taste like shit now," Rachel countered. "The new guys always skimp to cut costs. They say he doesn't even speak Cantonese."

"Yeah, well not all of us had parents with the foresight to teach us the language. And if you hate it that much, then why not just go to the one on Gerrard?"

"Is that place even still around? And I don't even remember the last time I crossed the Don. Can't have been since the revitalization work started . . . "

The sale of New Hong Fatt marked the third change of ownership and second location for the Chinatown establishment that had existed under that name for probably over a century now. Matt's gnen gnen still reminisced about the old location on Bay and Dundas from years back, before the city decided it needed to replace its Chinatown with a city hall and a section of its Jewish neighbourhood with an expressway.

Matt's gnen gnen also told stories about how the second owner of Hong Fatt BBQ did change the recipes to cut costs, and how the original owner had to come in and retrain him after too many people complained and then stopped going and it almost had to close. But once the second owner got their act together, the store was always busy, especially on Chinese New Year's Eve, when there were huge lineups that Matt's gnen gnen was somehow always able to cut. As a child, Matt had assumed his grandmother's ability to cut lines was part of some secret connections she had in Chinatown before he learned the real secret was to shop regularly and tip generously.

On a green light, Matt glanced around quickly before gunning across the intersection at Portland Street, his windshield glowing an angry red to protest his minor traffic violation. The arrival time counter in the upper right skipped down from 4 min to 2 min as he made the turn into the "delivery vehicle only" lane heading north on Spadina. Behind him, in the bed of the truck, a pair of wheeled, polished aluminum crates engraved with the words "FROOMBA™: Smart Crates" chirped and beeped as they rolled heavily to the side.

"Your mom's homemade stuff was pretty good."

Rachel was right. Matt's mom had come pretty close to replicating the marinade, but she didn't have the equipment to roast the pork at the proper temperature, and so in Matt's opinion it still never really came close to the real thing.

"Hey, you never tasted her first attempts. I can still feel in my mouth the taste of how dry that pork was."

Matt had gone deep into some grill and smoker forums one week and bought the materials for a DIY standing oven for his mom's seventieth birthday, but in the end he couldn't find someone who could weld. And anyway, his mom never really cooked in "that style" anymore, since produce prices had become so high.

Prices for Chinese veggies—and produce generally—shot up when Bob's Choice, one of the three major national grocery chains, bought and then immediately closed the Ontario Food Terminal, the publicly run supply hub that provided most of the independent Chinatown grocers with access to low-priced quality produce. The closure of the food terminal, along with a city-wide ban on single-use Styrofoam containers and plastic wrap, forced most of the grocers to shut their doors in turn as shoppers left for the nearby Fresh Basics, the discount brand of another major Canadian grocery chain. Over time, most of Chinatown's recognizable stores, banquet halls, eateries, and even the old family associations had closed or moved to the suburbs in search of cheaper rent. Gradually, the names that Matt's family used for their usual spots changed.

"Wanna go to Third Floor this weekend?" became "You know, the new AGO building," when the third-floor restaurant, where every week Matt's family gathered for dim sum, disappeared. Its building had been purchased by the well-intentioned Art Gallery of Ontario looking to expand its gift shop. The restaurant was turned into a Michelin Star dim-sum themed restaurant complete with cart service and featuring a rotating menu spotlighting a different area of China every month.

A few years before that, "The Lucky Moose had them on sale" had become "I was parked by the old moose," referring to the nineties-era moose statue that had stood in front of the former Lucky Moose Grocery by Dundas and Beverley. The old store was now boarded up and adorned with a faded mural depicting a bearded Prime Minister Justin Trudeau handing one of those life-size cheques to a smiling Gavin Easton Jr., heir of the Bob's Choice empire, both wearing surgical masks and looking in desperate need of a hairstylist. It was a shame most of the ten-dollar hair salons were also long closed.

Matt said goodbye to his cousin and then ran his hands through his hair and sighed as he thought about how much more expensive things were now. Glancing at the seat beside him, the e-paper display of an old children's novel flickered as the elderly man pictured on the cover, wearing a purple cloak with a long silver beard, waved. Suddenly the man reached off-page and took out a whole raw chicken, gesturing with his wand to conjure the words "11.99/lb – ONLY @ FRESH BASICS."

"Friggin ads, they're watching me," Matt mumbled as he flipped the book over. "The kids aren't gonna buy whole chickens . . . "

Matt turned the corner onto Grange, and then up Huron, passing the old Low Gong Association House where his mom served briefly as treasurer before its members voted to sell the house and disband the association. The opportunity to receive tens of thousands of dollars each was worth more than the prospect of an occasional association banquet and space to play mahjong. Across the street was now a blinding wall of glass.

In place of the old Chinatown, Bruegle, a large global tech firm, had set up a brand-new campus around their Canadian head office, surrounded by a technologically well-endowed mixed-use planned neighbourhood. The former heart of Chinatown was memorialized with a restaurant that was free for Bruegle staff but open to the public and featured chefs flown in from the Bruegle office in Beijing. The restaurant was decorated with gaudy red pillars and dragons and faux pagoda roofs over the cafeteria, all set inside the glass facade of its architecturally award-winning office. It was an impressive sight that doubled as a convenient advertisement for its food-delivery service, "Bruegle Chow," whose logo had been etched into the tall glass panels. The only reminders of the old Chinatown were the old folks selling home-grown gah and gai lan and 4lb buckets of SUPERIOR TOFU sitting in big tubs of ice water beneath the shining windows.

Matt pulled to a stop at the corner of Huron and Dundas, wheels just over the curb. The truck sounded its arrival and the windshield glowed to frame a comparatively modest, old, white-bricked building on the right as the destination.

"It looks exactly the same," Matt thought to himself as he climbed out of the truck, tapping his phone to order his FROOMBAs to unload from the back and follow him. He dug into his pocket for one of those old-school mechanical keys.

The red and white sign still read "NEW HONG FATT BBQ RESTAURANT" above the empty glass display where the roast pork and chicken and duck normally hung. Inside, the now-antique salmon tiled walls and green linoleum floors felt exactly like they had since the 1970s.

The only hint Matt could see of the change of ownership was a faded old photo pinned behind the counter, depicting Matt and his Mom smiling over a plate of homemade, visibly dry, BBQ pork on rice.

TIFFANY LAM

Tasty

2050 is the last year of the Cleanse. The Cleanse was a ten-year process. In 2049, they pulled the plug. All restaurants and markets on
Spadina Avenue—the life and blood of Toronto's Chinatown West—
were to close their doors.

The threat of COVID-19 never completely went away after 2020.
The tug-of-war between people who "needed" to leave their homes
and officials "recommending" people stay in meant outbreaks kept
happening. For thirty years, uncertainty over what exactly would help
control the virus remained a mystery to Toronto residents.

The virus's spread made less and less sense to epidemiologists
around the world. It was more mysterious than vape deaths. Its muta-
tion in 2048 created the most fear. No one knew how or why, but one
day, health officials determined that the virus *was* clinging to surfaces,
long enough to spread through intercontinental shipments. In the
past, the success of vaccines had reduced lots of COVID-19 infections
to the level of respiratory illnesses like the common cold or the flu,
but suddenly, infected people developed nasty pneumonia-like symp-
toms at a higher rate than before. Lungs gave up. Kidneys failed due
to aggressive medication. Strokes from near asphyxiation were also
a common cause of death, particularly for the elderly. The Ministry
of Health didn't need to call strokes COVID deaths though, which
meant underreporting the virus' death toll. People stayed quarantined
for months.

The Cleanse was introduced when all hope seemed lost. The

immunocompromised had died in great numbers. Birth rates plummeted due to rampant depression and fear. Low-income households continued to be disproportionately represented in essential and frontline jobs, leaving the most vulnerable communities the most exposed to the virus. Black homes mourned as institutions resisted collecting race-based COVID impact data that could help drive policy. Wages could not keep up with rent. Homeowners who relied on the rental market to support their mortgage payments faced foreclosures. People went homeless more than ever, while empty condos stared down from above.

The Cleanse was the response and today is Tasty's demolition day.

"Look at this. It's from the Toronto Preservation Board."

He looks down at the memo. It reads:

"In 2008, Council endorsed a values-based approach for heritage conservation with the adoption of The Standards and Guidelines for the Conservation of Historic Places in Canada as official policy for the conservation of heritage resources within the City of Toronto.

"Properties and Heritage Conservation Districts of potential cultural heritage value or interest will be identified and evaluated to determine their cultural heritage value or interest consistent with provincial regulations, where applicable, and will include consideration of cultural heritage values including design or physical value, historical or associative value, and contextual value. New applications are currently pending to recognize Toronto Chinatown West as a Heritage Conservation District and therefore immune to destruction."

Pending. After all that jargon, that was the word that stood out.

"What authority do they even have here?" he asks.

"Apparently, some," she says.

"Is this a joke? It's a rule from 2008. Things are different now."

"They've stopped shipping things from abroad. We told them those goods couldn't be trusted and they complied."

"Their margins failed the Assessment."

"They have a case that the strip has associative and contextual value."

"A filthy row of restaurants and wet markets has a case?" He's incredulous.

"Chief," she says, clearing her throat. "Chinese people have been living there for some time. Lots of people shop there. They eat there. It's a place for people to get together."

"There is no precedent for this. Plus, the Cleanse deemed it unviable; it's made its decision."

She sighs. "There are people sitting around the perimeter of one shop. The inside too. Blockading it from the trucks."

"They are out there right now?"

"Yes."

"Book them for not following Cleanse bylaws."

"They're sitting at a distance around the perimeter. And inside. Masked."

"Bastards. We can't even identify them then."

Masks must always be worn in public.

Tasty Fruit Market has been an unofficial symbol of Toronto's China-towns for many years. It always kept its produce affordable. It sold the best lychees, dragon eyes, and mangosteens. Mangoes are expensive everywhere else. Passionfruit and durian are the slowest to sell but at least they would sweeten. Despite the name, Tasty sold things other than fruit too: gailan, watercress, the hair vegetable for New Year's, dried noodles, fresh noodles, goji berries for aunties' soups, real vinegar for dumplings. The best thing about it was how you could pick ingredients for someone there to cook them for you. You could grab a quick bite sitting at one of the assorted plastic stools parked at mismatched plastic tables. People bought beer and stayed until closing. It was the closest thing to a night market you could get in Toronto.

The Cleanse rolled out in two five-year phases. Phase One assessed supply chains around the world for how they fed into Toronto. It confirmed that the virus's origins were outside the country. With the virus clinging to surfaces, supply chains were disrupted. Directives mandated going local. Restaurants and markets in Chinatown that relied on imports were hit hard. Companies were then subject to Phase Two,

The Assessment. The Assessment gave businesses a chance to rejig their operations and examined how much revenue a business brought in and whether they contributed to the GDP. Companies were valued at how much they contributed to the COVID economy. Of course, mom-and-pop shops in Toronto's Chinatowns struggled to meet those margins, especially since one global power in particular continued to perpetuate the narrative that "The Chinese" were to blame for the virus in the first place.

Before Phase One started, Tasty began preparing to grow produce it would not be able to import anymore.

The headlights of the demolition vehicle cut deep. Some idiot just kept it idling, exhaust leaking into the sky. The wrecking ball is not as big as I thought. It's pure steel and motionless but menacing. A handful of by-law officers are around but they have nothing on us. They just stare and stew in their lack of authority.

There are about eighty of us sitting around Tasty's perimeter in the blazing heat. People have lined up against the wall. Some start inching towards the shade. A group of local bros are laughing at themselves for being in "chinaman" squats. "It's not racist, because we're saying it! 哈哈哈哈哈~"

I wonder if that's true and go inside.

Another twenty people are gathered inside, six feet away from each other in their imaginary personal bubbles. Out of the corner of my eye, I see a bougie girl eyeing the duller, admittedly grimier parts of the mint linoleum floor. I think she's contemplating popping a squat herself but first assessing the dirt she would be coming into closer contact with. We've been here almost seven hours now, so I understand. I wonder if she's come here because she knew somebody who wanted to be here.

Either way, I'm appreciative. Without the crowd, they would have dispersed us easily. Tasty has been my family's for so long. I don't remember life without it. It's a stubborn little place that has refused to shut down, despite barely making a profit. This was always the idea: grow our own food, sell enough to buy some things, and sustain the people around us. I got us a liquor license, so people could get a drink with their fresh food, and it became hip to eat here. It really hurt to think that The Cleanse would take it all away so suddenly. I can't help but feel that it is targeting Chinese Canadians.

It's funny, I didn't even want to take over Tasty in 2020. I had lost my Air Canada job as an attendant when flights got cancelled. Coming out of my undergrad a few years before, it was tough to figure out what I could do with an arts degree in Chinese and French literature. Being a flight attendant seemed like the only place to apply a degree in foreign languages. It was nice for a while. I got to see places. Then COVID hit and arts skills were tougher to sell than ever. My parents invited me to come back here because they really needed the help. Out of nowhere, something I had vowed never to do—take over the family grocery business with a fobby name—kept me afloat and connected to a community.

I hear an engine rev up and all the chit chatter ends inside Tasty. I run outside.

A guy in business casual is talking to Guo. Guo beckons me over.

"Is everything alright here?" I ask.

"We're leaving," says Business Casual.

My face lights up. *Did the application work?*

Business Casual turns around and blows the corniest whistle to tell some guy to get back in the truck. Engines rev again and the dump trucks back out. The crane and wrecking ball follow. The whole squad shuffles away.

"How—?"

"They will probably be back tomorrow, which means so will we," Guo says. "But the crew will leave us tonight. I reasoned with them."

He winks and it dawns on me that I've never seen his face.

I shake my head and chuckle. "With how much?"

RAZAN SAMARA

Planting Seeds

For a while, we were winning, or at least it felt like it. We knew progress wasn't linear, we had to make sacrifices, endure losses, and work towards it each and every moment of our numbered days. It seemed that the masses were finally listening to us, to repetitive history, to the signs in the earth, water, air, and fire. But it wasn't enough. The Giants (the corporate powers), afraid to lose their stance, assumed a defensive position; they gave way to the demands of the working class, but just enough for us to taste the sweetness of the fruit we had painstakingly grown. Many of us were like those who fast from sunrise to sunset, filling the hole in our stomachs with a single meal, failing to recognize fleeting pleasure from meaningful change. There were, however, a few of us who dared to reach for more, but we were met by gatekeepers. We tugged and we pulled, but they claimed our tree wasn't ready for harvest. They pruned the maturing tree and covered its exposed roots with soil, insisting they were caring for it. The Giants knew how to hide their intentions behind magnificent foliage. They encased the tree in glass and laid down a commemorative plaque, claiming to protect it from the elements, but we knew this to be just an attempt to separate it from the garden it had come from.

Amali woke up to the sound of a plate shattering. She groaned face down into her pillow, knowing exactly what had happened. With a sigh she stood up on her bed, hands on her hips in a judgmental stance. She looked down at the remains of the plate of sliced fruits her mother had brought her the night before while she was studying. Moments ago, it was haphazardly balancing on the edge of her bed. She took two steps back, feeling the mattress sink under the weight of her body, then one step forward before leaping to the other side of the room.

She landed on her feet and turned around to face the mess between her and her bed. She got down on her knees and picked up pieces of white ceramic and ageing apple slices, balancing them in her small palms as she tiptoed out of her room and into the kitchen to dispose of them. She washed her hands under warm water, picking out the soft brown flesh of the apples from underneath her overgrown nails. I don't even like apples, she thought to herself.

Pools of sunlight were starting to fill the two-bedroom apartment, light glistening off countertops and knickknacks that her mother meticulously kept clean. The small unit was tucked away in one of the last standing low-rise buildings in the city, but even her twenty-two years showed more on Amali than a century did on her home. Her mother walked into the kitchen and opened a window, letting the faint buzz of traffic from Bathurst Street enter. "You fell asleep in your bed with a plate, didn't you?"

Amali smiled to herself, her silence confirming the early morning event. She knew her mother was being cheeky, so she waited for the "I told you so."

"Your alarm didn't go off," she added.

Amali thought for a moment. "I must've fallen asleep before setting one."

Her mother pulled her into an embrace with one hand, the other gently brushing out the tangled curls in her hair. "Then perhaps you can blame fate this time. The plate could've fallen at any moment in the night, and yet it fell when you were supposed to wake up." Amali held onto her mother a little tighter, taking in a breath of her honey-suckle-scented skin for safekeeping. She was nervous about the day ahead of her—in a mere couple of hours she would write the last exam for her undergraduate degree, but the hints of honey and ripe citrus always calmed her. Her mother knew, of course, so she was soft on her this morning.

She thought she would feel lighter, but something was off. Amali took a short cut through campus on her way home from finishing her exam, walking through the grass field in front of Convocation Hall where she would be graduating in a couple weeks. She had always admired the rotunda's architecture; it was a welcome break from the high-rise complexes that dominated every block between the grounds of the university and her neighbourhood opposite the Toronto Western Hospital.

She turned right onto College Street, then left onto Spadina to make her way down to Dundas. Her quick, decisive steps were slowed down by crowds of people aggregating in front of her. It was an unusual amount of foot traffic, even for one of the busiest areas in the city. She found herself on the road as the crowds spilled beyond the sidewalks. She watched as the streetcars slowed down to a halt. There must be an accident up ahead, she thought. She forced herself forward through the crowd.

Amali's heart began to race as she reached the front. This can't be an accident, she thought. Then she saw the dozens of bodies lying on the ground, all clothed in black. Some lay on top of one another. Are they alive? How did—Her thoughts were disrupted as a young woman in black pushed past her. The woman stopped for a split second, intensely locking her brown eyes with Amali's, before rushing away into the centre of the scene. She looked not much older than Amali and, given their similar features, she could've been Amali's shadow breaking off from the crowd. She went and lay down on her back and crossed her hands in front of her chest in a rehearsed manner. A few others from the surrounding crowd ran to join her.

A few moments passed, then like clockwork, the bodies in black rose to their feet. They locked arms and began chanting. "No justice, no peace! No justice, no peace! The end of capitalism is here!" Police officers in bulletproof vests and gas masks suddenly flooded the scene, some of them carrying sniper rifles in their hands. The armed police tried to break up the crowd, pulling people apart and dragging them on the ground. Amali's cheeks were soaked with tears, something in the air was making it hard to breathe. She pulled her t-shirt over her nose and ran to hide in an alleyway a few blocks down, the same direction she had come from. She sat down and rested her back against the wall, taking in deep breaths with her eyes closed, they were red and irritated. She heard two shots from a distance. She had never heard a gun before.

She counted five minutes' worth of seconds in her head before opening her eyes. At 60 seconds, hurried updates from a police radio echoed in the alleyway. At 100 seconds, the police van doors slammed shut one after the other. At 180 seconds, the sirens began to grow distant. At 240 seconds, the streetcars' familiar hum ramped up again. When Amali opened her eyes and peeked out of the alley, it looked as if nothing had happened.

Amali fumbled with her keys, finally finding the correct twist at the same time her mother swung the door open from the inside.

"Where were you? Why didn't you answer my calls?"

The tone stung like acid, all the sweetness from the morning gone. Amali rushed into the living room to turn on the television, swiping her hands rapidly over the holographic screen to advance from one news channel to the other, looking for images of the bodies in black and the officers in riot gear. Nothing.

Her mother stood in the living room waiting for an answer and beginning to lose her patience. "Amali, why aren't you answering me?"

Amali clenched her fist, struggling to control her frustration. She wanted to tell her mother what had happened, but she wasn't sure if her words would be enough. "There was a demonstration, or maybe it was a protest. I'm not really sure what to call it . . . but there were these people, and they were all wearing black, just lying on the ground and on top of one another. They closed an entire intersection at Spadina and Dundas. And then they all got up and started chanting. Then the cops came, wearing bulletproof vests and gas masks, some of them with sniper rifles. They threw tear gas grenades and started arresting everyone they could. I didn't realize how close I was, standing there until my eyes started swelling up." Amali took a deep breath and rubbed her eyes, but her mother's alarmed expression signaled she needed to take a longer pause.

Her mother was rarely this quiet. They both stood still in the middle of the living room, the faint voice of a news anchor filling the silence.

"In the last twelve hours panicked investors have withdrawn over twenty billion dollars from money market accounts. Typically seen as a low-risk savings option for short-term investments, consumer confidence in the accounts plummeted as news came that the National Bank of Canada had filed for bankruptcy early this morning," reported the anchor.

Amali's mother hovered towards the TV and turned up the volume. She sat down on the sofa and motioned to Amali to sit beside her. They watched the TV together as a parade of suits and dress shirts projected in the air.

"It is no secret that the National Bank of Canada was in deep trouble, it has been for most of the past decade. When the majority of your clients have a history of debt and poor credit scores, then offering them mortgages is risky. The borrowers defaulted. We've seen this play before, but that doesn't mean the impact will be the same as before—this is a disproportionate reaction," explained a commentator.

"The National Bank of Canada's prominence has steadily declined over the years. In no way does it compete with the Big Five banks, who are the ones holding our economy together. This is just a blip in the system. In an electronic marketplace, things change instantly. So this may feel like a blow, but I assure you, it is not. Trust the system, put all your trust in it. Together, we will prosper, but not without your confid—"

The projection disappeared, cutting off the slogan of the New Economics Party, the current party in power. Amali's mother put down the remote and they sat together in what felt like endless silence.

It all sounded too familiar. And yet it wasn't like anything Amali had ever experienced in her lifetime. She had never witnessed protests. Her encounters with politics until this point had been limited to films and textbooks.

Her mother asked her to describe the demonstration again, this time intervening with careful questions.

"Were they wearing any symbols, perhaps something that looked like an hourglass? Was there anyone who looked like they could be leading? What did they look like? Did you see anyone you recognized?"

Amali was surprised by her mother's inquiries. With each question, she wondered if there was knowledge her mother hadn't shared with Amali before. But her mother offered only more questions, and between the impassioned cries at the protest and the cold voices of the men on the TV, Amali wasn't sure how she should feel. As she tried to make sense of it all, she realized that mostly she was confused. And then came a loud growl from inside her. She was hungry.

Her mother took notice and ended her barrage with a nod. She began to busy herself in the kitchen, chopping onions, tomatoes, and bell peppers with practiced precision.

Now that her mother was calm in her natural element, Amali wondered if it was her turn to ask questions. She nervously hovered around her mother, waiting for the right moment to interject.

"Mama, have you ever seen or been to a protest?"

Her mother caught her eye for a moment before returning her attention to the simmering sauce and cracking two eggs to complete the shakshuka, a breakfast dish they'd routinely turned to for comforting late-night suppers. Amali paid no attention to the tangy aroma, patiently waited for her mother to reveal something new to her.

"Well, when I was your age, it was legal to protest. It was our right to demand better, to claim power for communities. So I've been to a couple, yes, but it was a long time ago. Everything is different now."

There was a bitterness in her tone.

"What did you protest for?"

"There were many reasons, many different reasons . . . we advocated for immigrant rights, climate justice . . . we tried to address violence and demanded safer communities."

"Who's 'we'? And what kind of violence? How come you've never told me this before?"

Her mother sighed. "Amali, it's been a long day, khalas."

Enough? Amali thought that unfair. But she knew she couldn't push her mother any further. She had said the magic word, which could put an end to any conversation.

The rain beat gently against Amali's window as she woke up from her sleep. Still drowsy, she caught sight of her alarm clock. It read one pm. She jolted up, her remaining sleep evaporating off her as she rushed to change into her day clothes and tidy her room. What a mess, she thought.

She made her way to the kitchen to make herself some breakfast. She thought of her mother as she made a grilled akkawi cheese sandwich. Her mother was working the day shift at the hospital and was probably having lunch with some other nurses on a break. Amali plopped herself on the living room sofa, her sandwich in one hand and the other gesturing at the TV as she switched between her Social Circle feed and news channels to check for coverage of the demonstration. Still nothing. She wasn't surprised by her social media feed, nothing violent or antigovernment could ever leak past the censorship algorithms. Amali couldn't recall any other demonstration in the city. They were forbidden, along with any gathering that wasn't preapproved by the Public Events Committee. It seemed strange that not even local news outlets had picked up a story this unique. She switched to the channel again, happening upon the hourly economic forecast. The consumer confidence barometer captured her attention immediately—she had never seen it that low.

"Consumer confidence has fallen to the lowest level in a decade . . . The Big Five banks and the Federal Government are reassuring Canadians that the economy is strong, and they should continue investing and spending. This is particularly important as demand for the Canadian dollar in the global market continues to drop against a strengthening euro . . . Economists warn of a devastating chain reaction if consumer confidence and spending, which drives ninety percent of the country's economy, continues to fall."

The details were foggy, but one thing was clear: the more money people spent, and the more that was invested, the better was the economy. The New Economics Party had nearly no control over the market. It relied heavily on corporations making a profit and the confidence of consumers to grow the economy. Amali was taught that the system could be trusted; after all, the economic conditions did improve when the New Economics Party took power following the devastation of the 2020 Pandemic. So, what was happening now?

Her thoughts began to cluster as her mind drifted to the pandemic, then to her mother and the little glimpse into her past that she had gotten the night before. She had always been curious about her mother's life, it wasn't often that she was able to get details from her. Amali knew it was difficult for her mother to share her stories. Feelings of loss and sacrifice were deeply embedded in her memories.

Amali knew very little about her mother's parents, other than that they came to Toronto as refugees from Palestine with her mother, then a toddler, in tow. Longing for their homeland, her parents returned to their native city of Nablus after her mother graduated from nursing school. Amali's mother chose to stay in Toronto, thinking she would be able to visit them the following summer. Then the pandemic hit and both parents passed away. As Amali's mother was recruited to the frontlines, she worried about her elderly parents being all on their own. It was only after six years that borders reopened and Amali's mother was able to visit her parents' tombstones among Nablus's rolling hills.

Warm tears streamed down Amali's cheeks, dripping onto albums and scrapbooks. She looked for photographs of her grandparents to appease her sudden need to imagine what they would've looked like if she had ever met them. She thought of her mother's pain and all the stories she could've shared with Amali if not for the sorrow she carried inside her. Among the photos she found was one of her grandmother stitching an embroidery pattern. Her hands looked as tense and concentrated as her facial expression. Amali shuffled through the pile and came across another photo of her grandmother. This time her face had a lighter expression as she sifted through oranges in an open-air market. Amali's tears turned into broken laughter as she noticed her grandfather at the edge of the frame, about to take a giant bite of a banh mi sandwich. She flipped the photograph to read her mother's faded note: Elham and Samer, Chinatown 2019.

It had been years since Amali last thought of Chinatown. She had photographs of herself as a toddler there, dressed in a puffy winter jacket and knit hat, standing in front of what looked like hundreds of lanterns for a Lunar New Year celebration. She thought about the possibility of standing in the exact same spot as her grandparents that summer day, between rows of ripening oranges and soft bananas, somehow still connected yet decades apart. By the time Amali had been old enough to put together two words, nearly every small business in Chinatown had been uprooted to make way for residential developments and corporate offices. Long gone were the dim sum restaurants, independent markets, and local vendors of the photographs.

Amali tried to imagine her family's memories in an attempt to construct a timeline of her own. Feelings of rage consumed her as she held the images of faces and places in her hands, feeling robbed of stories she'd never heard. She thought of how her mother always made sure not to reveal too much.

The evening glow lit up the living room with sun-soaked yellows and blood oranges. Soon her mother would return home, bringing with her the city's exhaustion. She would greet Amali and catch her up on her day, but only take a moment of rest before getting busy again with the next thing. Amali continued to sort through the photographs, paying close attention to the ones that reminded her that her mother had once been young too. Many of them had short notes upon them, offering some insight into her mother's world. One photograph, however, had a particularly long passage written on the back.

> We will be known as a culture that feared death and adored power, that tried to vanquish insecurity for the few and cared little for the penury of the many. We will be known as a culture that taught and rewarded the amassing of things, that spoke little if at all about the quality of life for people (other people), for dogs, for rivers. All the

world, in our eyes, they will say, was a commodity. And
they will say that this structure was held together politi-
cally, which it was, and they will say also that our politics
was no more than an apparatus to accommodate the feel-
ings of the heart, and that the heart, in those days, was
small, and hard, and full of meanness. —Mary Oliver,
"Of The Empire"

Amali became still. A moment passed, then two. She couldn't care for time anymore, feeling it wrap in and out of itself, trying to escape the bounds of an irreversible succession. She felt she had been offered an understanding from the past. She read the words again, revealing to her her mother's secrets. What happened then? Are we any different now?

The poem burned into her mind as her fingertips traced over the glossy colours that immortalized her mother huddling closely with friends on a couch. Their smiles looked unencumbered, but their tired eyes hinted at a different reality. Amali held onto the photo, unsure of what to do with it, but knowing it couldn't return to its hiding place.

On cue, her mother made her way through the front door. She puffed out a greeting, glanced at the sprawled photographs for a split second before making a beeline for the kitchen. She began to preoccupy herself with washing some of the vegetables she had bought on her way home. Amali walked over to the kitchen counter, attempted small talk about her work; but her mother sensed that Amali was only setting her up for a different conversation.

"The same as usual. What were you up to today? I see you've been busy making a mess in the living room—do clean that up soon, habibti."

Her emotions raw and the photograph still in her hand, Amali decided she couldn't wait for the prime trifecta of mood, time, and place to open up a conversation.

"I was looking for photos of tayta and sido, and I came across this photo of you and some friends. You wrote a poem on the back—do you remember it?"

Amali's mother glanced at the photo and sighed. "I do, yes. It's still one of my favourite poems. Mary Oliver was brilliant; this was one of her lesser-known poems. I believe I have one of her books somewhere if you want it. Did you find photos of your tayta and sido?"

"I did, yeah. There was a really funny one of sido eating a sandwich while tayta was buying oranges in Chinatown. You took that photo, right?"

Her mother laughed softly. "Yes, I did. Your grandparents loved Chinatown and the community there; we visited nearly every day. Your tayta refused to get her groceries anywhere else."

"Why was that?"

"It was her way of showing solidarity. My parents lived as aliens while they were here, they didn't have any other place that reminded them of home. Your sido would also never turn down an opportunity to eat dim sum, he probably missed Asian food more than me when they moved back to Palestine."

There was a glimmer in her eyes as she pointed to the photo in Amali's hand. "That photo was taken in Chinatown too. I'd meet up with my friends in the basement of the Dragon City Mall. It was a special place."

Amali felt a knot tighten in her chest. She had spent so much time being angry at her mother for shutting her off that when she did share pieces of her life, Amali didn't quite know how to handle it. She felt her mother's openness and was afraid that her next question might inhibit it.

"Mama, last night you mentioned that you used to go to protests. Was this something that was a big part of your life? Was it something you did with your friends? I just don't feel like you tell me anything. How am I supposed to know you? How am I supposed to remember you? And tayta and sido? I just want to understand."

The knot loosened in her chest. Amali looked down at the photograph, hesitant to make eye contact with her mother. Shit, did I go too far?

Her mother walked over to the photographs lying sprawled across the floor. She dropped her hands from her waist and took a deep breath. "In school, they taught you about the 2020 Pandemic and every year they held assemblies commemorating the lives lost. But your teachers, they never talked about everything. I've been waiting to share this story with you, and perhaps I waited too long. You know that period was a defining moment in my life. I was the same age as you now, becoming an adult in a world I didn't even recognize anymore. Everything changed, from the way we experienced birth to how we mourned the dead. And as devastating as it was, it also felt like an opportunity for communities to reflect and connect, to grow into what we wanted to be, rather than what we used to be. As we came close to the 2023 Federal elections, people were yearning for change, to improve their circumstances. That's when the New Economics Party was born and where your school lesson ended, but the story is far from complete without mention of the Sovereignty Uprising."

Amali listened attentively. She had never heard of the Sovereignty Uprising before. She nodded silently to confirm her mother's assertions, not wanting to impede her flow.

"When the economic impact of the pandemic began to hit, governments chose profit over people and the environment. It was just another turn in a vicious cycle of harm. Leaders, activists, and organizers rallied together. My friends and I, along with our neighbours, we'd come together in that basement at Dragon City Mall, and we asked ourselves: what are we willing to give up to save a single life? A thousand lives? Millions of lives?

"The Sovereignty Uprising was a response to the oppression of Indigenous communities, heightened anti-Asian sentiment, and the Black Lives Matter movement. It was during the early days of the pandemic and long before the New Economics Party came to be. We were advocating radical change in every system that governed us. We were united in reimagining a shift of power to communities. We had to make sacrifices. We had to give up ideas that we may have benefited from in the past, like capitalism, because it always came at the expense of others."

"So, the demonstration in the city the other day—do you think it was an echo of the Sovereignty Uprising?" asked Amali.

"I wouldn't be surprised if that was the case. The Uprising never ended; attention just shifted elsewhere. We had strong support, but when the economy showed signs of collapse, people were overcome with fear. They worried about industries shutting down and losing their jobs and homes—their ability to sustain themselves and their families. The New Economics Party took advantage of that fear, it promised that people would have nothing to worry about as long as the economy was strengthened. And in order to do that, they needed people to invest back in the economy."

Amali recalled the Party's slogan: "Together, we will prosper, but not without your confidence."

Amali's mother nodded. "A lot of people were skeptical about their intentions, but the thing about capitalism is that despite its deep roots in oppression and white supremacy, it was familiar and comfortable to people. Instead of giving it up, the New Economics Party gave it a new look. They and the banks and corporations aligned themselves with the Uprising, mostly performatively, to gain trust. When they had won the election, the Party started to show its true colours—but it was too late. They needed people to spend, even if it meant accumulating debt. The culture of capitalism became even more pervasive, making it a dominant force in everyone's lives. Under the Party's mandate, the economy seemed to recover, but that came at the cost of an increasing social divide and the devastation of the environment. Their motives were in fact to strengthen corporate power."

The Giants, Amali thought. They were the corporate powers in her mother's story. The Giants were the companies credited with saving the industries after the Pandemic, and now they monopolized the markets. Amali had always thought this made things simple—there was no competition or comparison to be made. Instead, everything had its place. Suddenly it felt like nothing was ever that simple.

The demonstration. The bankruptcy. The investments. The Uprising. The Party. The Giants. Amali's mind flitted from one thought to another. Her mother's articulation was overwhelming. They rarely had conversations of this sort.

The background city buzz turned into a quiet hum, introducing a noticeable lightness into the evening. As Amali and her mother shuffled through the photographs together, sharing memories and anecdotes. Amali learned about Raven and Omar, the two friends pictured in her mother's photograph. Together, they had volunteered with the community at Dragon City Mall to organize community-care initiatives. The trio always had fun, however, often racing around the city on bikes to see who could deliver the most care packages. When protests eventually became a daily occurrence, Amali's mother began volunteering as a first responder. She mentioned marches attended by the thousands and long nights at encampments. Though her mother was exhausted, Amali couldn't help her curiosity.

"What did tayta and sido think of all this? Were they worried about you?"

Her mother took a moment, pulling herself away from distant memories and back into reality. "They worried as all parents would, but your tayta and sido were disrupters. They went back to Palestine not just because they missed their homeland, but because their existence there was a form of resistance against the Israeli occupation. Resistance runs through our lineage. I know they feared for my safety, but I also know they were proud of me for standing up for what was right."

Her mother held her eyes with a soft smile, reaching to brush a tangle out from Amali's hair with her fingers. "I know it's taken a long time for me to share these stories with you, and there's so much more I want to share with you. Just not right now, not all at once. I'm proud of you, and the kind and compassionate person that you are. Things are beginning to change, and it's going to be confusing, but you must make your own choices and stand your ground like my parents did, like I did. I know you'll always do what's right."

Amali had always rushed through the corporate business district (CBD), paying little attention to the identical skyscrapers, or their thousands of inhabitants who always seemed to be on a call or vigorously typing on their phones. Everything and everyone always looked the same. Walking through the CBD now, Amali tried to imagine the Chinatown in the photographs, with lit-up signs welcoming passersby into restaurants and herbal remedy shops, and colourful baskets of fruits and vegetables lining the sidewalks. She wondered what had happened to the displaced businesses and families.

She had stayed up all night researching the Sovereignty Uprising and Chinatown, finding few traces of her mother and the community's history. What she did find was overwhelmingly sympathetic to the New Economics Party, so much so that it felt suspicious. But she also found an address for Dragon City Mall. Finally letting herself rest, she dreamt of visiting the place where so many of her mother's stories originated.

Standing in front of the mall now, she realized that she had passed by the unassuming building thousands of times before but had never thought to step inside. It was on the corner of the intersection, flanked by two corporate high-rise towers. She looked up at the pedestrian bridge connecting the twin towers from twenty stories in the air, then back down at the five-storeyed Dragon City Mall, where it sat in its rightful place and yet looking out of place. She wondered how the building had survived all these years.

Amali circled the block, contemplating if she should go in or not. She watched the entrance as people went in and out, some leaving the building with tote bags of groceries slung over their shoulders, others holding take-out boxes and little brown paper bags in their hands. She finally stepped inside the building. She was welcomed first by the warm aroma of Hong Kong egg waffles from a small stall on her left, then she noticed a rather unusual quietness in the mall. Even the groups of Chinese-speaking elders were conversing in hushed voices, maintaining the generous silence while socializing around small tables.

The midday sun streamed in through the glass entrance, nourishing a tree blooming with flowers and tiny unripened oranges at the centre of the mall. With only its trunk and branches in view, it seemed to rise from the lower level through an opening. For a second Amali wondered if it was synthetic, but then she picked up the notes of citrus in the air.

While it looked recently renovated, the peculiar architecture and selection of businesses hinted at a much deeper history. Art-adorned freshly painted white walls and grey quartz tiles paved the floors of a small lobby before branching out into two corridors of storefronts depicted in languages she couldn't read. The lobby opened up to a cross-section view of the upper-level floors of the mall. From her vantage point, Amali could see more restaurants, stalls, and shops on the second floor, while the third seemed to be exclusively for medical services.

The mall interior seemed to create its own climate and Amali was lost in its atmosphere. She was pulled back from her trance when an elderly lady softly elbowed her with a look of disapproval, motioning Amali to move away from the front entrance. Amali moved forward until she reached a glass railing overlooking the lower level and the base of the orange tree. She could now see it stood nearly thirty feet tall.

She stayed by the railing and the oranges, unsure of where else to go. There was a staircase on her right and an escalator on her left, both leading to the upper levels, but the lower level seemed to have less obvious access. She circled around the mall, looking for anything that reminded her of scenes from mother's photographs. Feeling lost and out of place, she prayed for a sign.

Amali wandered aimlessly around the lower level, feeling tired and foolish for letting photos of a room from two decades ago guide her. What am I even looking for? Preoccupied with her thoughts, she began to make her way back upstairs when a lively hello startled her from behind. Amali turned around to see a woman staring directly at her, her brown eyes holding hers in a familiar gaze she couldn't quite place.

"I saw you at the protest last week. You're here for the meeting, right?" The woman turned and began walking, calling out over her shoulder, "Come on, we're both really late."

She's the one who bumped into me at the protest. There was something about her presence that made Amali instinctively follow her down the corridor to a storefront with a closed security gate. Amali watched her pull the gate open, just enough for her body to disappear inside. Amali peered through the narrow opening and saw people gathered inside. A couple of dozen people were sitting in a circle on the ground, listening to an elder. The elder's voice was soft and unwavering. Amali stood at the back, wondering what she would have to give up to cross the threshold into the unexpected.

AMY YAN

Chinatown Island

Ma Ma says that we used to live in Chinatown. That our house near the corner of Boulton Avenue and Gerrard Street used to be at the heart of at what was the city's Chinatown East.

"I know this area used to be Chinatown East, before the pandemic changed everything," I say as we cross to the south side of Gerrard and Broadview on our way home from the park. "But really, Ma Ma? This used to be a Chinatown?" I had seen pictures of Chinatowns of the past in my history books from school, but our neighbourhood looked nothing like those pictures.

"Yes," replied Ma Ma in Mandarin. She always uses Mandarin even though I only want her to talk to me in English. "Zhōng Huā Mén Gate stood on the corner of that block right there," she says, pointing to where an e-bike repair shop now stands. She points south down Broadview. "Urban Outfitters down there used to be a Chinese herbal medicine store. Wai Po always went there to get her red dates. And that vintage record store on Gerrard was an open grocery market. They always sold the best white radishes."

"What was that store then?" I giggle and point to the newly opened VaporLyfe! on the other side of Gerrard Street, knowing that it would set her off. Ma Ma had been strongly against the opening of the new "poison store" (as she put it in Chinese) in our neighbourhood last year, with its flashy hologram window display and bright neon green lights. Without fail, she would bemoan its presence every time we passed it on our way to the park. "We should have moved a long time ago," she would mutter under her breath. "We don't belong here anymore."

"That used to be Leung's BBQ Shop," she said, an edge in her voice. "Mr Leung actually was one of your Wai Gong's friends."

"What was—"

"Mi Mi, another time, I will answer your questions. But right now, we should hurry home."

"Ma Ma!" I yelled when I got home from school the following day. "I have a field trip form for you to sign!"

Ma Ma emerged from her small home office with a sigh. She looked tired and had her long hair swept up in a tight bun on top of her head. Whenever she did this, I could not help but notice all the white hairs she had hidden in the layers below. She pushed her large glasses up her nose and looked disappointingly at me. "How many times have I asked you to keep your voice down when I am working?" she said. "I could have been in a meeting."

"Sorry," I said and swiped the screen of my school tablet in her direction, sending her the form. "I wanted to make sure I didn't forget. We're going on a field trip tomorrow and I need you to sign this so I can go."

"To Chinatown Island?" Ma Ma asked, pulling the form up on her watch and reading the hologram display that popped up.

"Yea, you've never taken me there before and Ms Britton is gonna make us write a paragraph on why Chinatown Island is important."

"I don't think you're ready to go tomorrow," Ma Ma said.

"But why?!"

"Because you don't know what Chinatown Island is yet."

"Yes, I do! We learned all about it in history class today." I took a deep breath, ready to impress Ma Ma with everything I had learned that day. "The 2020 Pandemic caused all of the small shops in the old Chinatowns to go out of business because people weren't allowed to go out and buy anything in person. This caused all the old China-towns to close down and the Chinatown BIA didn't know what to do because there was nobody that could stay open after the pandemic ended. So they got together and decided to create a whole new, awesome-er Chinatown on the old Toronto Islands and they put cooler things in it, like a giant lucky-cat hotel (that has a moving arm!) and a whole bunch of cool carnival rides so that people can go there whenever they want and enjoy the China theme park and drink bubble tea and eat Chinese food and also see a super big Chinatown Gate replica. So there! I know about all of it. Please can I go tomorrow, Ma Ma?!"

"No," said Ma Ma.

"Aaargh! Just let me go!"

"No," repeated Ma Ma. "That is not what Chinatown Island is."

"But it is! That's what we learned in class," I protested.

"Chinatown Island is not a bigger, better Chinatown, Mi Mi. When I was a little girl, Chinatown was a place where I could go and feel like myself. Why do you think Wai Po and Wai Gong decided to live here, where Chinatown East was, when they first came to Canada?"

"But can't you still feel like yourself while you are having fun?"

"Sure," said Ma Ma, "but the fun is making you forget why Chinatown Island was built in the first place. It wasn't built for us, it was built to seem like it was for us. After the pandemic, the city's Chinatowns couldn't sustain themselves anymore, but Toronto needed a place that still seemed like Chinatown and still was a place that people wanted to go to. When the BIA backed the project in an attempt to relocate some of their businesses, it made Chinatown Island look even better."

"But if some original shops moved there, doesn't it make it the same, just in a different place?"

"Leung's BBQ was actually one of the shops to move," responded Ma Ma quietly. "Your Wai Gong told me that it was really hard on Mr Leung, but in the end, he had to go or the business would go under, and he had to support his family. But the shop was never the same after the move, no more roast duck and pig hanging in the windows. They even stopped making it for a while."

"Why?"

"Because they wanted to avoid anything that would scare away customers who were not Chinese, and everybody was worried about cleanliness at the time," said Ma Ma. "But a Chinatown is not a theme park, no matter how successful Chinatown Island has ended up becoming. Chinatown is a place where we can feel like we belong. And I can't feel like I belong there."

I sat down for a second, unable to respond.

"Do you understand now, Mi Mi?" Ma Ma asked.

I nodded slowly, knowing that any sign of me not understanding would send Ma Ma into another long explanation.

"If you understand, then I suppose I can let you go tomorrow," continued Ma Ma, signing the form with her finger and swiping it back to me. "But just remember, Mi Mi, Chinatown Island is not what you think it is."

I practically skipped off the ferry as it docked itself on Chinatown Island the following afternoon.

"Where do you think you are going, Minnie?" yelled Ms Britton breathlessly as she struggled to get herself down the ramp, one hand on the handrail and the other gripping her purse and marking bag bulging with assignments she had been grading on the ferry ride over. She was a large old woman who always seemed to wear the same flower-pattern skirt and open-toed sandals year round. She lumbered off the ferry with the rest of the class trailing behind her. "I want us all to stay as a group until I have done a final headcount and set up our field-trip trackers. There are just too many people here and I don't want anyone to get lost."

Ms Britton then proceeded to shepherd us to a small grassy area off the main path to do a roll call. Once she'd done that, she flipped open her marking bag and produced a large electronic tablet and a handful of blinking bracelets. "Now," she said with a huff, "time to set up your field-trip trackers to make sure I can keep an eye on you all as you do your exploring. I've never had to set this up before, so you all shall have to bear with me." She then began fiddling with the buttons on the display. "These darn things," I heard her mutter under her breath, as all the bracelets suddenly stopped blinking and the display began making an alarm sound. "We never had to use these back in my day."

While Ms Britton struggled with her tablet, I took the time to look around. We were still on the edge of the island, in the tree-dotted belt of grass that ran all the way around its perimeter. The main attractions were further down the path that started from the ferry docks and bisected the island.

It was already afternoon, but many tourists were still coming off the ferry and heading along the path to the centre of the island, with cameras and maps pulled up on their hologram watches. I shivered in excitement when I saw the top of Lucky Cat Hotel peeping above the trees from where we stood. I could almost smell the xiǎo chī that I knew vendors sold further down along the path.

"Minnie, are you listening to me?" Ms Britton sounded annoyed. She was standing before me with a tracking bracelet in one hand and the other hand on her hip. "This is important, Minnie, I need you to listen to me and I won't repeat myself again. This bracelet is the only way I can monitor you while you are exploring the island. We're here for only a couple of hours and when it's time for us to go home, the bracelet will buzz. You must come back to this spot, do you understand?"

"Yes, Ms Britton," I said, as she slipped the bracelet over my hand and tightened it on my wrist.

"All right!" said Ms Britton, turning back to the rest of the class. "You may go explore now. Remember to think about why Chinatown Island is important for your essay tomorrow!" But by this time we had already deserted her, running down the path to the heart of the island.

At first, Chinatown Island was everything I thought it would be. Ma Ma's words of caution did not even cross my mind as I rounded a bend in the path and the heart of Chinatown Island lay before me.

On either side of the path, extending a full block in length, were small storefronts, before which the vendors had spread out their goods. There was a store for jiǎn zhǐ, outside of which an elderly ā yi was demonstrating an intricate paper-cutting pattern to a rapt crowd of tourists. There was a store for Chinese ceramics: blue and white vases, sets of colourful rice bowls and soup spoons, all on display behind the glass storefront window. There was a souvenir shop selling every conceivable red item, from collapsible paper lanterns to fridge magnets to calendars. There was too much on display to take in all at once. And of course, there were the food stores! As I walked along the path, food aromas wafted towards me: the milky smell of bubble tea, the eggy goodness of freshly baked tarts and buns, the comforting fragrance of fried rice.

Finally, I fixed eyes upon the carnival further down.

At its entrance stood Chinatown Island Gate, an exact replica of Zhōng Huā Mén that had once stood at Gerrard and Broadview in our neighbourhood. Its green pagoda roof stood out above the trees around it and two stately lion statues stood on guard before its three arches. A dragon-shaped rollercoaster cart, complete with flowing whiskers and moulded scales, suddenly soared into view behind the gate, riding on flaming red rails through the air. Just next to it a large carnival wheel with golden spokes and lantern-shaped seats rotated rhythmically around a flashing five-pointed star. The wheel slowed down, the ride came to an end, and the passengers were let off, seat by seat.

It was all so colourful and bright that for the first few minutes I simply stood there and watched. Another group of people got on the Ferris wheel and the lanterns started to make their way around again. The dragon coaster looped around itself and the passengers screamed loudly, lifting their arms up in the air. The Lucky Cat Hotel, visible in the distance, had its large face pointed east and its giant arm waving slowly like an inverted pendulum. A pattern soon started to form: the Ferris wheel would come to a stop as the dragon coaster launched itself into the air, excited tourists would get on and off the rides and wander back down the path, all while the Lucky Cat waved its paw back and forth unceasingly.

But gradually my excitement began to wane. I started to feel that the whole scene was somehow unfamiliar. The lanterns, the dragons, the Lucky Cat—they were all things I had seen or heard about from Ma Ma before. They were not foreign to me. But seeing them all come together in the form of a carnival made them somehow unrecognizable.

I tried to shrug this feeling off, remembering how much I had wanted to come here. It probably was just that I had been staring at the same thing for too long.

Leaving the carnival area, I decided to head back and get something to eat. I remembered smelling freshly baked egg tarts on my way to the Ferris wheel and my mouth watered. As I went about searching for the bakery, I saw two of my classmates standing in front of a store-front window, intently looking at something inside. I went closer and saw that they were looking into the window of a BBQ shop. Just inside the window hung eight perfectly roasted ducks, their crispy golden brown skins shiny with grease. Below them hung several strips of chā shāo, from which excess fat was dripping into a steel pan. But both these sights paled compared to the roasted pig that was dangling on a large hook by its hind legs, the crackly crisp skin on its back facing out towards the street.

I had only ever seen such window displays in history books and in pictures that Ma Ma had shown me from her childhood in China-town East. There were so few people who knew how to make Chinese BBQ now in the city—the tradition had pretty much stopped after the pandemic—that Ma Ma only went through the trouble of getting roast duck or pork when there was a special occasion in the family. And she had to drive all the way out to Scarborough (where one small shop still operated) in order to get it. But the store never had its products hung up in the windows.

As I stood admiring the hanging meats, I overheard my classmates as they chatted.

"It's so weird . . . "

"You can still see the eyes and ears!"

I wanted to tell them that it wasn't weird and that it tasted really good. I had always looked forward to the occasions when Ma Ma would make the trip to Scarborough and bring back takeout boxes full of the delicious meats. But before I could say anything they turned to me.

"Do you eat that?" one of them asked pointedly.

What she had said was not particularly unkind, but they were standing together and I was on my own. I could feel a heat of embarrassment rising up from my cheeks to my ears.

"Y-yea, I have," I stammered, "I've tried it before."

"Ewww," said the other. She jammed her finger into the window, pointing at the pig. "Have you tried to eat the head?"

"I mean, we don't usually—" I began. Ma Ma's words came back into my mind. I can't feel like I belong there, she had said. I glanced towards them again and suddenly felt as though I was on display. That all the things I had grown up with were on an overproduced show for tourists to gawk at, and that somehow I was a part of the attraction. Was this the same feeling I had felt by the carnival rides?

"Can I help you?" A deep voice sounded suddenly from beside me. I whipped around to see a tall Chinese man standing in the doorway of the shop. He looked to be about Ma Ma's age and wore a chef's outfit and hat, with a grease-stained white apron around his waist. He looked towards my two classmates.

They froze.

"Um, no sir!" they said in unison. They quickly backed away from the window and disappeared into the crowds.

The man turned to me.

"Oh," I said, "I was just admiring your window display. I've only seen a BBQ window display like yours in books."

"Yep," he replied proudly, "I decided to start setting up the window display only a little while ago. My father never did it after the pandemic, but I thought that it was time. Before then, I had only seen them in books too."

I nodded. It certainly was an impressive display. I then noticed the monogram on his shirt: Leung's BBQ. "Wait," I asked, "is this Leung's BBQ from the old Chinatown East?"

"Yes, it is!" the man replied, surprised. "How do you know about that?"

"My mom told me that you used to be located right by Broadview and Gerrard," I said, "and she said that my Wai Gong used to be friends with Mr Leung."

"Really! How fortunate you've dropped by. No one your age has ever brought up Chinatown East to me before." He was clearly impressed. "I am Charlie Leung, and Mr Leung was my dad. He was the one who moved us here after the pandemic shut down Chinatown East. Why don't you come in and take a look?"

He opened the door wider and rich aromas of Chinese BBQ welcomed me inside.

I can't quite remember how long I spent in the store. Once I was inside, Mr Leung offered me some duck and pork from the window, and while I ate (and complimented him on how good it tasted) he started explaining some parts of the store to me. He began to prep slabs of raw pork for the following day, using his family's secret mix of ingredients, all the while talking to me about some of his experiences growing up and working on the island. He was so friendly and open that after I had finished eating (and tried to pay him for the food unsuccessfully), I found myself asking if I could help with the cooking. "Oh, really, you don't have to," he said. Then seeing my insistence, he continued, "but if you really want to, you can help me wash and prep the vegetables. We have our monthly vendor-gathering today and I could use some help with the side dishes."

"What's the monthly gathering?" I asked, as I took off my tracking bracelet and placed it on the counter so it wouldn't get wet as I washed the vegetables.

"My dad liked to host a small get-together for the other vendors each month," he replied. "It was his way of saying thanks to the community, and so I continue it now that I've taken over. Leung's BBQ would have gone under a long time ago if it wasn't for the support of the other vendors on the island. I guess porcelain bowls and jiǎn zhǐ are just more palatable to the tourists than what I've got to offer."

I nodded silently. I got started on washing the lotus roots, white radishes, green onions, and a myriad other vegetables that he laid out, like I had so often done for Ma Ma at home and, when she was still alive, my Wai Po. It was something I had always loved to do. Back then, I would have to stand on a stool to reach the sink to scrub the vegetables before handing them one by one to Wai Po to chop up. It was a ritual I always thought of as private, something of ours that my family had kept up after the pandemic wiped out so much of our space from the city.

Even though I was born long after the pandemic, over the years Ma Ma had managed to convey to me the loss she had seen and felt, and so to some extent I felt that loss too, although I'd never let myself get too bothered by it. In school it was easy to ignore the fact that I was Chinese. Diversity and inclusion were ideas constantly preached in class, but I would also just never bring up anything that I knew the others didn't know. It was easier that way; they wouldn't feel awkward and I wouldn't feel different. Which was why I was so confused that I was finding myself feeling so at home in the very same place where, just moments earlier, I had been pointed out as different in a way I had no control over.

It wasn't until Mr Leung started cooking the vegetables on the stove and asked me if my parents knew where I was that I remembered my tracking bracelet. I ran over to where it lay on the counter. It must have been buzzing for a long time because it was now completely out of battery. "I was here with my class. I should have gone back when my bracelet buzzed, but I forgot!" I said hurriedly. I looked out the window and panicked when I saw that the crowds of tourists had thinned significantly and that long shadows were already starting to stretch along the path. "They must have gone! What time is it now?"

"It's 6:34." Mr Leung replied, quickly turning off the stove and walking me to the door. "The Island will close pretty soon, at seven pm. I really am sorry that I kept you so long, I should have asked you earlier, but I got caught up in my stories."

I dashed outside with Mr Leung following. I was hoping to see the shape of Ms Britton in her flower-print skirt somewhere along the path, but also knew too well that she had probably left with the rest of the class hours ago. As I stepped outside, I heard a voice calling my name and suddenly, out of nowhere, hands grabbed me by the shoulders and spun me around. I looked up and was amazed to see Ma Ma, a worried look on her face. Her eyes scanned me up and down to make sure I was all right. She hugged me close to her and then quickly pulled away. "Mi Mi," she began angrily in Mandarin, "what were you thinking? You had me so worried! Why didn't you listen to Ms Britton and go back when you were supposed to?"

"But Ma Ma—" I began.

"No," interrupted Ma Ma, "I knew I should not have let you come here in the first place. Where were you this whole time? Your school had to be alerted and we've been looking all over for you!"

"She was with me," said Mr Leung, cutting in from behind me. "I'm so sorry, but I was showing your daughter my store and lost track of time. It's my fault that she missed going back to her class."

Ma Ma looked towards him, anger and confusion on her face. But her eyes landed on the monogram on his shirt and her expression shifted suddenly. "Charlie Leung?" she said.

"That's me," Mr Leung said a bit sheepishly, a look of surprise also flashing across his face. "I recognize you now. You must be Annie. Your dad used to bring you all the time to my Ba's store in Chinatown East."

"That's right. I can't believe you're still here. I mean, I knew that your dad moved the business here after the pandemic. But—" Ma Ma's eyes drifted behind Mr Leung to the display I had marveled at earlier. "How is this here?" she gasped in surprise. "After the businesses moved, my Ba said that it was all gone, and the whole store had changed. I've never seen a window display like this since I was a little girl."

"Yes, it was very different after we moved here," Mr Leung replied quietly. "My Ba had the hardest time with all the new rules that were set out for Chinatown Island. He had to change everything about the way he ran his business in order to stay operational. And he couldn't bear the sight of those rides as they were being built." He gestured towards Chinatown Gate and the carnival area. "They have never belonged to us. They were always for the tourists."

"They're superficial," agreed Ma Ma. "I've never wanted to visit Chinatown Island because of that. I wouldn't have let Mi Mi come if it wasn't for her field trip."

"But, you know, my Ba was never superficial," said Mr Leung softly.

"Yes, he had to do things to stay in business, but he never forgot who he was and neither did any of the other vendors. They all remembered what Chinatown was supposed to be, and as long as that stays the same, we can still find community in each other. That's something that the pandemic can't take away."

I looked around me on the path of Chinatown Island. The lights in the carnival area had been turned off and, with the rides now shrouded in shadow, the shops stood out against the fading light. The vendors and their families were all busily taking down their displays for the evening. Warm lights shone from inside the shops as they chatted in Chinese to their neighbours about their day and helped each other pack up. An elderly couple walked down the center of the path and waved at Mr Leung. "We're coming over for the meeting soon!" they called and Mr Leung waved back. I recognized the elderly woman as the ā yi who I had seen earlier in the day at the jiǎn zhǐ store.

I looked at Ma Ma and saw her gazing around her. There was a look in her eyes that I hadn't seen before. A sense of belonging that was never there when she looked at any other place in the city.

"Well," she said after a long pause, "I think it's time to go, Mi Mi. It's late."

"Will we come back, Ma Ma?"

"Yes, Mi Mi. Very soon."

EVELINE LAM

Interval

Auntie, family friends would hiss, *was a disgrace. All that work into funding her retirement*, they would go on, *and for what? For her to leave after two years and slum it in Chinatown?* Tongues clicked like mahjong tiles.

While I had cheerfully yelled *goodbye!* from the car window when we left Auntie at the retirement home years ago, all this gossip had left the memory foggy with embarrassment. And so, seeing her again leaning over the counter of a grocery store, I couldn't bring myself to say hello. She was haggling over the price of the oranges she'd brought to the counter, asking for *ordinary ones*, as though bruised fruit was common to see. The shopkeeper barely hid his irritation, *lady, if you don't want to pay this price, someone else will.*

Auntie sighed and began to turn around, abandoning the produce on the counter. She caught my gaze and I was trapped, though I could do nothing but avert my eyes as she walked past. I assured myself that there was no way she recognized me, but the thumping in my chest told me that I just hoped she didn't.

She left the store.

I didn't follow.

I spent much of my life putting things in order. Each day I rose early and worked the morning quarter inputting data for the Societal Resource Planning department. And in-between, I completed my physical maintenance exercises. The first day of the week brought a replenishment of my food stores according to my consumption data. All meals were perfectly attuned to my preferences, and even the smallest craving was met with exacting attention, like last Thursday when I found 35 grams of cereal packed in a fresh-seal bag.

But it was twelve pm on the first day of the week and there was no nutrition box inside my mail pantry. I double checked that I was hungry, and I was. So I stood there, looking at the spot where I should have seen a perfectly portioned lunch. The conditioning system hummed to itself and the screens blinked languidly, but their beeping sounded as confused as I was.

Wait, beeping? Startled, I scurried over to the monitor at the entrance. Clearly something had not synced properly with the last software update.

I stuck my thumb onto the wall and waited for the system to recognize my fingerprint. The wall blinked and filled with the message:

RENEW BIOMETRICS

Oh. Of course. I've had the same fingerprints for twenty-four years, yet the Service Center requires every registered citizen to do a yearly full-body scan, otherwise services get put on hold. I dreaded this annual pilgrimage. The Center always said that technology made things easier and better for us, that we were free to do anything only when everything was automated. Even though I heard this many times, there was still something about this errand that felt unnatural. I tapped the wall anxiously: I wasn't prepared to leave my apartment.

I spent the day opening and closing the pantry door, willing the food to come, hoping that the system was wrong. But the system is never wrong. The next morning my stomach started aching, and I gave in, realizing I wouldn't get anything done without submitting my fingerprints. With a final grumble, I turned the door knob.

Billboards refreshed themselves as I walked down Spadina Avenue. They flicked between smiling women and bright monochrome signs, cheerful and placid, but with no text except for brand names. I saw that the phone I'd bought two weeks ago had a next-gen version and wondered if I should buy that one too, since mine didn't come in the "Baby Boy Blue" Pantone Colour of the Year. While many people turned their ad blocker on when they went out, I only left my apartment once or twice a year and couldn't justify the subscription. It never took up more than thirty-five percent of my peripheral vision anyway.

Although the renewal center was in Liberty Village, I took a detour to go review D'Arcy Bakery in Chinatown. I had complained to my friends on the building forum about my software update and they told me I might as well continue my work for the Tastemaker programme, as in-person reviews were worth double the points. The shop wasn't yet popular enough to hit the daily feed, but I had a hunch that in a week's time, my photos would be reposted and the prices would skyrocket.

I rarely came down to Chinatown anymore, even though the bright yellow pagodas and hand-painted signs made it a popular backdrop. Red lanterns swung between posts crawling with steely-eyed dragons and the stone lions lined up at the edge of Huron plaza. The city had widened the sidewalks and removed street parking a few years back, but the slew of amateur photographers and tourists with extra-long tele-lenses still made the neighbourhood feel overpacked. The only Asian faces I saw were behind the storefronts.

My mom had grown up a few intersections away from Chinatown on Markham Street, and she often told me about the evenings after work when she would go out of her way to buy groceries at the open-air market. She would be jostled by employees pushing carts of *gai lan* and squeeze her way down the narrow aisles, caught between aunties in wide-brimmed hats and cans of straw mushrooms. She always smiled when reminiscing about the old Chinatown, though she inevitably ended every story with, "Thank goodness they'd cleaned up those streets, it was so dirty."

Those words sounded strangely out of place, and I wondered whether they were really hers. She would turn away and hide her expression, busying herself with wiping the countertop or some other chore.

Passing by grocer display fronts, I could smell that the scent of the week was based on the month's top flavour profile "Old Spice," although I could not recall the names of any of the spices. The scent never corresponded with the produce that was piled high outside in their containers. You weren't supposed to shop here: the glass jars of dried cordyceps and foam-filled boxes of dragon fruit were for display only.

There was a steady stream of couriers coming and going from the pickup counter, clutching bags to their chests. The low-touch order stations glowed softly, illuminating the faces of the patrons as though looking into the shifting, watery depths of a pool. I couldn't remember the last time I'd stood in a line. Once I got my delivery service set up, it had reduced my time spent and food uneaten in such a drastic way that it felt wasteful to go and pick out my food.

This is when I had noticed Auntie, a figure who stood out for how utterly unremarkable she looked. Wearing pants with faded polka dots and a striped shirt a size too big, she moved with disarming carelessness. And I found myself standing behind her, a spectator to this pantomime of a time long past when people would go buy groceries.

It turns out that she had left the store only to patiently wait for me on the busy street corner. *Hello*, I finally said when she reached out and took my hand.

There are certain people you imagine surrounding yourself with: young tech entrepreneurs in their Tesla model Bs, indie influencers who post photos of their trips sponsored by the Amalfi Coast. Then there are those, like Auntie, whom you cross the street to avoid, pity filling the space between. This time though, I don't know why, I closed that distance and let her small, wiry fingers grip mine.

There was nothing but squat grey apartment blocks in Alexandra Park and I started to feel that Auntie was taking me to see these alleys full of nothing but dead ends. For a moment, I considered leaving to pick up a dozen Juicy dumplings for $8 to eat on my couch—wouldn't it be easier to watch a show about family bonding than to really do it? At least I could turn it off at the end of forty-five minutes.

Then she abruptly stopped short at the edge of an open field and I fell forward—just as I realized, upon closer inspection, that the field was made of chives. The slender stalks reached towards the clouds and waved drowsily in the breeze, small violet flowers grasping at the sky. Auntie kept going and I could see, all the way to the horizon, the wind ripple through the chives just as a wave crests in the ocean. We kept moving, half submerged in the field, until the ground dropped out beneath our feet: a square hole, five by five metres. A red ladder stood just high enough above the edge. With all the strength of her sixty-eight years, Auntie grabbed the first rung and disappeared below the earth. I followed.

In the first sunken courtyard, the sky appeared closer than ever, as though it were painted on the ceiling of this room in the earth. I could hear voices—lively, happy, angry conversations—and as I followed Auntie through the shadowed hallway to the next open court, I found a multitude of people trading stories and food, couples linking arms on brightly upholstered benches, and men in flannel shirts clinking tea cups. Dialects wove in and out of each other, sometimes three different languages making up a single sentence.

It was odd to see real faces. I saw my friends every day, but they were glass figures with tinny speaker voices. But these people, it seemed, lived their days in close proximity: words and gifts and food spilling over into each other's spaces like overgrown vines, trading seeds of ideas and thoughts, allowing roots to grow and link them together.

A man gestured at a pot of soy milk on the counter, ready to be ladled into tiny paper cups. I stopped at his stall and tried to order. My speech was halting, and I felt my cheeks colour. I was repeating the same basic phrases in Cantonese and though I rolled the words around in my mouth to smooth them, when they fell from my lips, they felt jagged and coarse.

The heady smell of charred *siu mei* wafted around me, seeping into my clothes; the scent of smoke would linger long after I got home. The air felt like the breath of a mythical beast, a pulsing source of heat and singed meat. Two steps forward and the smoke was cut by an ocean spray, a salty taste that lingered like foam flung from tide pools. Mismatched bottles filled with fish sauce were lined up on the back shelves, sharply amber when hit by sunlight, pungent and still in the shadows.

While Auntie was preoccupied with the vendors, I peered past her shoulder at another courtyard. It seemed more private, more serene. I could see fields of lettuce shivering in the wind, guarded by rows of cabbage sentries in their green and maroon uniforms. Tomatoes hung like lanterns above a drowsy crowd of potatoes and yams sleeping beneath a blanket of soil. Buckets of mint were sequestered in the furthest corner, no doubt an attempt at thwarting their unceasing invasion of all other garden plots.

I'd only ever seen these items lined up in neat shop displays or in padded boxes.

Auntie had set down on the counter a pomegranate, a bowl of water, and a small silver paring knife. She deftly scored the skin and, gripping the halves with her fingertips, cracked open the fruit. I was shocked by the bright red flesh and the starkness of the rind reminiscent of grinning teeth. Tiny droplets spilled out from the cut and the juice ran down her hands, blooming in the water. Auntie's clean gestures conveyed the confidence of a butcher.

She plucked a single seed from the bloody water and offered it to me. My hand jerked away and hers flinched too, disappointed but not surprised. I leaned forward while she pulled back, *no no, it's okay,* as our hands reached towards this seed that was now the hinge around which our bodies swiveled. I felt the frustration twist my face, and only then did I realize I could stop chasing, that I didn't need to be constantly winning, that I could simply be willing. So I stopped, turned my palms up, and simply asked, *please, Auntie?* And she, too, stopped resisting. She placed the seed in my palm. Though still wary of my reaction, she busied herself again with the remnants of the fruit and I took a second to examine the tiny jewel.

There was a deep crimson spot at the heart of the seed, capped with a little peak of snow. I felt as though I were holding an entire world within my hand. I placed it gingerly between my teeth and bit down—a burst of juice spurted on my tongue. The tartness seeped in and my taste buds were roused, unable to distinguish between sweetness and discomfort. I smiled as I reached out and asked for more.

Auntie takes me back to the spot on Dundas Street where the road curves around the hospital vents. The sun sets the clouds alight and drops of colour splatter onto the pavement, looking like streaks of neon dropping from the sky.

She hugs me and I hold onto the foreign, familiar feeling as I head home to my high-rise box. I feel displaced, as though I'd just woken up in a stranger's bed more comfortable than my own. I cannot shake the fear that I have been a fool and bartered my freedom for convenience. If enlightenment is a Google search away, how many more will give me what Auntie has given in a day: the pleasure of being misunderstood? What a joy to explain myself, to open myself to the potential of other people.

Up above, the drones make their last eight pm sweep, stitching together a digital record of the city grid, taking no notice of the lives below.

ROBERT TIN

Porcelain

Toronto, 2050

Noah? Noah, wake up. Please take your vitamins while I initiate the shower.

"Yes, mom."

This is a single-room suite equipped with a kitchenette and a bathroom. The room is dressed in all white. The space is kept dark, lit only by a desk lamp and the illuminating signs and digital billboards across the street. The diverse colours of the outside disperse and tinge the cold white room as they enter. A clear glass of water sits on the icy quartz countertop. In the Petri dish beside it are two white chalky capsules. A tall slender figure wraps his long boney fingers around the glass of water. His complexion is so pale that the refraction from the glass makes his skin glow. He pops the capsules in his mouth and shoots his head back, gulping down the pills.

Noah has been taking these so-called vitamins ever since he can remember. He has no idea what they are; they boost his immune system, he supposes. It has never come to his mind to question what they do or why he has to take them. It is just a routine in life.

Noah? The shower is ready.

Noah automatically makes his way toward the sound of the water. This is his favourite part of the day. It is the only time something dynamic makes intimate contact with his body. Water is his best friend. He loves the way it dances on his skin. He loves the way it relaxes him. He loves the way it drowns out his thoughts.

It stimulates his senses; he was taught that it also keeps all bad things out. Bad things such as the monsters his mom used to mention in bedtime stories. They would haunt him as a child. They were imperceivable and had the abilities to possess him, causing great suffering, and ultimately, death. The way the water coats his skin feels like an embrace that comforts and protects him.

He also loves how unpredictably water behaves and wishes he could also move freely like water, melt away into the drain to see where it goes. He wonders what it is like beyond the confinement of his apartment.

"Mom, can you tell me about the world today?"

Sure I can, Noah. Elixir, the newly developed condominium, has started construction in Chinatown today . . .

Noah takes a deep breath as he sheds his all-white comfort wear. He puts on his full-face snorkel mask before stepping into the shower.

. . . This will be the twenty-fourth building of the redevelopment project of Toronto's Chinatown in partnership with the Tech company, Curbside Labs.

Protests rallied outside City Hall today with over ninety people wielding banners urging the City Council to fully pay for and provide medication to every citizen in Toronto . . .

Ever since COVID-19, people have been living in caution and fear. It's been a never-ending battle that's exhausted everyone's body and soul. It became apparent that the virus was never going to be completely defeated. Despite everyone's best efforts, they could only develop a preventive drug with seventy percent effectiveness. Now everyone is advised by the Ministry of Health to take one pill every day. "Advised," as supplies are scarce, and many people in Ontario do not have access to it. In Toronto, the municipal government has also increased the amount of chlorine in the water supply to battle viral diseases and bacterial infections. It seems to have a particular effect on the skin, turning it lighter. There have been multiple cases of mass poisoning, the toxin level in the water having become too high. Therefore it has become standard practice for Torontonians to boil their water for at least 30 mins before consumption.

The government knows that sacrifices must be made for the bigger picture, despite the numbers of outraged citizens questioning this practice. Given the choices, it would take the easiest option within its jurisdiction. A government only governs those who are living; COVID-19 has been nothing but death. It does not like it when something is not within its control. It would much prefer to be the sole entity to decide the life and death of its people. Government obsession with total control is why another global catastrophe happened shortly after COVID-19: WWIII.

. . . conflicts in numerous communities in Toronto suburbs. Seven people have been hospitalized with 1 person in critical condition. No arrests have been made.

There had been a breach of security in the central server—

Noah, would you like me to continue?

There is no answer. Noah can only hear his thoughts, the rest of the world muffled with the sound of the falling water.

NOAH-3003

I am Noah.

I was born in March 2030.
I live in Toronto.
I am a Canadian.

I find my day to be quite mundane:
Eat. Sleep. Shower. And maintain.
I listen to what mom tells me to do and behave,
every day since blood first coursed through my veins.

She only has to say the words and my body will move.
I can't get through a day without her telling me what to do.
It's not the instructions; I am stuck in the same old groove.
I just feel safer when I have someone to fall back to.

Although it has already been ingrained,

I can feel this routine slowly turning me insane.
Sometimes I have trouble suppressing my brain,
Thoughts keep telling me to break free and be unchained.

But I can't. I was raised by mom's voice; I live by her words.
If she heard my thoughts, she would really be hurt.
I'm scared she'll find out as she knows everything in the world.
It's best that I keep my urges furled and stowed.

She once told me that my first word was "mom."
She has taught me everything I know except for where I came from.
Her sounds are never just noise, there is always meaning in them.
I can still faintly hear her voice, even when water falls head to bum.
The murmur of the water provides me with balm.
I envy the water that escapes my palm.
Just as it has my mind enthralled,
I can hear my mother's call.

Noah?

Noah?

I can't imagine life without mom's voice.

Noah?

I can't imagine life without mom calling my name.

Noah?

Noah?

I can't imagine someone else calling my name.

Noah?

Noah?

Noah?

I cannot imagine someone else.
I cannot imagine life otherwise.
I . . . really can't.

There must be more.
More to this world.
Just like there is more to me that I don't know.

Noah?

I take off my mask.

"Noah." I say out loud.

The shower stops and the room speaks back to me in my voice:

Noah . . .

Noa . . .

No . . .

N . . .

Wowar-3 Aka The 2nd Wave

After the pandemic, Western nations placed the blame for its spread on China. Harsh words volleyed back and forth over a series of press conferences. Foreign relations had never been more tense. Eventually they led to war.

WWIII is not traditional warfare. It is not a war for conquest, nor is it a war for freedom. It is an existential conflict. It would appear that the East and West cannot coexist as globalization continues to accelerate. This is a war for cultural dominance. This war was bound to happen, and COVID-19 was the reagent. There is no clear indication of when the war started. It is an unconventional war, cultural warfare. Many do not even know they are at war until after they have had a role in it. For this war transcends nations, it is fought by civilians. This war transcends physicality and materials. It is a war fought with danger-ous ideas and hurtful words. It is psychological. To the soldiers, this is the war they are destined to fight. Not only were they born with weapons, they were born with their team colours.

Over the years, the Canadian government has sought hard to main-tain its neutral middle ground globally. It has promised to maintain its role in the world's peacekeeping force. However, unnoticed by the government's all-seeing eyes are the divisions that have started to rip apart the unity of different communities within Canada. They have not realized that their people have enlisted in a war against each other.

Asian Canadians are the Huns, the common enemies of other Canadians to let out their frustrations, their rage for what has hap-pened. Other Canadians cannot accept the fact that the thing that has killed and tortured their loved ones does not have a face. They have decided that Asians resemble the virus more closely than they them-selves. They have replaced a pandemic by creating another, known as racism. Thus, Asians have been pushed away and scolded.

It is the little daily racist remarks that hurt the most. They are undetectable and go unpunished. In most cases, the people on the receiving end can only shrug them off. Little by little, the insults turn into gestures, and gestures turn into actions. It didn't take long for these to turn into targeted assaults.

Businesses in Toronto's Chinatowns have been hit the hardest. They were in the crosshairs for arson, theft, and vandalism early on. This eventually reached the point where there were more crimes than customers in the Chinatowns. Businesses started folding. By 2024, the last Asian Canadian-owned store in East Chinatown had gone vacant. Once East Chinatown was no more, Heritage Toronto scavenged the area for samples and artifacts to be archived. The following year the area officially got rid of its East Chinatown alias. Toronto now has only one Chinatown.

Canada portrays itself to be a place strong and united, intolerant of prejudice and discrimination. The more the reality strays from that ideal, the more people migrate further away from Canada. Noticing

this trend, the government of Canada came up with the idea of pre-
serving its people and its ideal image the same way it preserves its
chosen heritage. A nationwide initiative was started to preserve,
protect, and inoculate a select group of people from physical viruses
such as COVID-19, and mental viruses such as racism. The government believed that as difference creates conflicts, isolation eliminates
differences. And so, if everyone were in a world of their own, each of
them, along with their individual qualities, would be preserved and
not destroyed by conflicts. Every month of every year since 2030, a
newborn has been chosen at random to be added to this program,
which is now referred to as the Porcelain Project, and its participants,
the Porcelain Children. These ideal specimens will be the final frontier that upholds said Canadian ideals.

Noah is one of the first to be the last of his kind.

Pill #11011

Noah? Noah, wake up. Please take your vitamins while I initiate the
shower.

Noah's eyes open to the snowy white ceiling. His ears slowly become
aware of the white noise in the room. With a yawn, Noah gets out of
bed. He slowly drags himself over to the kitchen counter. Déjà vu.

Noah stares at the pills in his hand. He is sick. He is sick of rou-
tines. He is sick of repetition. He is sick of taking these vitamins.
Who knows how many of these pills he has already taken . . . He
wonders what would happen if he stopped taking them for once. He
wonders what would happen if he stopped what he is supposed to
be doing. He wonders what would happen if he stopped listening to
mom . . . Another day, perhaps. Noah takes the pills.

Noah peers out the window. It is quiet outside. The view looks like a
still image: an empty street with no movement.

He carefully scans the buildings across the street. They look exactly
the same as any other day. Noah squints to examine the digital billboards and the signs on them. He does not recognize the symbols on

a few. They look like drawings of little buildings. The outside world intrigues Noah. It's colourful yet lifeless. It's disorganized yet clean. Everything looks tiny yet vast. To Noah, the outside sometimes looks like a miniature model. It is so precious and fragile that it needs to be contained within a glass display case. It's hard to imagine that all the things his mom told him have happened in such a little space.

Noah finds himself lost in the details of the outside scenery.

A good fifteen minutes have passed. He wonders why mom has not told him to get into the shower yet. He does not hear water falling.

"Mom?"

No answer.

"Mom?"

Nothing.

Noah paces around the room.

"Mom?"

Still nothing.

Noah anxiously looks around the room. He is looking for his mom. He realizes he is looking for someone he has never seen.

"Mom?"

Noah closes his eyes. He listens closely.

Hmmmm . . .

"Mom?"

Hmmmm . . .

Only mechanical humming.

"Mom?"

He waits, hoping his mom's voice will break the silence.

Another five minutes pass.

Hopeless, Noah opens his eyes. He drops to his chair, unable to make sense of the unusual absence of his mom's voice.

Then Noah notices something, a slit of light around the front door. The front door has never been open, ever. He approaches the anomaly and is surprised to find that it is unlocked. He gently swings it open.

Noah finds himself standing in the middle of a long white hallway.

"Mom?"

The word did not come out of Noah's mouth. Noah finally hears a voice but it is not the one he was searching for. It is a voice he has never heard before.

Family Of Three

It is a breezy morning with light showers in mid-March, 2030.

Abel is putting on a hectic scene in the kitchen. It is his first time making dumplings from scratch. His wife Ella has been craving them ever since giving birth to their firstborn.

Abel is covered head to toe in white flour. With a rolling pin in his hands, he flattens out a stack of dumpling wrappers from a piece of dough that he evenly divided. He then scoops out a spoonful of filling prepared earlier and places it in the centre of a wrapper. He dips his fingers in a bowl of water. With care, he folds the wrapper in half to form a little pocket and seals it by folding the lips in an accordion pattern. First one done. A little deformed, but close enough.

Ella comes down the stairs cradling the baby in her arms. The baby is tightly wrapped inside a bunch of blankets . . . so small and precious. Seeing the disproportionate amount of mess Abel has caused just to make a few dumplings, Ella shakes her head and teases Abel with a smirk. Abel smiles shyly and defensively.

"It's harder than it looks."

"I know." Ella sits on the couch, lovingly watching her baby sleep. "I didn't say anything."

The pot of water on the stovetop starts to boil as Abel finishes wrapping the last dumpling. The dumplings vary in size, with a clear distinction between the first and the last one he's made. The first ones are packed to the point of bursting, while the last ones are less bulky with nicely sealed wrappers. Abel opens the pot lid, moving his head to avoid the steam. He slowly drops the dumpling piece by piece into the pot. The dumplings start rolling around in the churning water.

He sets a timer and leaves the dumplings to cook. As he walks toward his wife and his son, there is a knock on the door. Abel goes to answer. Two people dressed in medical masks and surgical scrubs are standing at the door.

"Can I help you?"

Without answering, they shove the door open and bash into the house. Abel is flung back against the wall. He looks down at himself and realizes he's been stabbed. The intruders go further inside the house.

"No . . . STOP . . . Don't go in there, you BASTARDS!" Abel roars at them at the top of his lungs. That took all the air out of him. Losing his balance, he stumbles into the kitchen. He fumbles for the kitchen knife. He knocks over a few things before finding its handle.

His mind is working faster than his body can react. His heart races in panic.

"Stop!" he growls, as he feels a piercing pain in his abdomen. Somehow he's able to stand up. He manages to find the back of one of the intruders. Abel points his knife to the intruder's throat from behind. "Leave," he warns, "the cops are on their way." The other intruder slowly turns around putting their hands up.

"Let him go and we will leave," the intruder's scratchy voice is muffled under the mask. "Don't hurt him, all right? Just put the knife down."

"We will leave . . . just let me go . . . !" the one under Abel's knife-point adds frantically.

Abel lowers his knife, letting the intruder go. He cautiously watches them run out the front door. Abel closes the door. It's finally safe. He lurches towards the living room. "El—" Ella and the baby are the only ones in Abel's mind right now. "Everything's okay. It's safe now."

As Abel reaches the living room, he feels a sharp object driven into his back.

"My name is Cain. No hard feelings. We are just here to clean up and take back our country," the third intruder says from behind Abel as he stabs him another time.

The knife has gone in deep. Abel's clothes are soaked in blood. He feels weak. He is angry, shocked, and desperate. He uses all that's left in him to try to hold Cain back from hurting his family. He doesn't want anything else but for his loved ones to be safe, to give his life for them so they can escape. Cain pushes Abel away. "Fucking pig," Cain snarls in revulsion as he swings his fist at Abel.

Abel falls to the floor. He puts his trembling hand over his stab wounds. "Ella, RUN!" He helplessly looks on as Cain enters his living room. RUN, he mouths. He is losing his breath. He is calling for help but his voice no longer comes out. He can only hear his pounding heartbeat and Ella's screaming in the distance. The house quickly falls into silence.

When the police officers arrive, the floor is covered in specks of glass and shards of porcelain. In the kitchen, the dumplings have been cooked into a thick porridge cake with a hint of char. The timer beside the stove is still chiming.

The officers follow a trail of blood into the living room. They find two bodies on the floor, their hands clutched together. They hear a baby's cry from under a pile of throws and cushions in a laundry basket. They quickly rummage through it. The baby stops crying as they pick him up to comfort him. As the officers turn around, they are startled to find a bloody maple leaf crudely painted on the wall.

Friendship 101

"Mom?"

My eyes meet with another's. This is my first time seeing someone else in the flesh.

"Mom?" The stranger repeats.

"Me?" I am confused. I clear my throat before stumbling over my words, "No, I'm not. I'm searching for my mom too, d-do you know her?"

"No." He replies, visibly disappointed at my answer.

We stare at each other for another long second. Not another word between us. I am mesmerized by his dark brown eyes. They are beautiful. I can almost see my reflection through them. He is looking at me the same way, deep into my eyes . . . until he blinks. He looks friendly, I think. He is also dressed in white. Except, unlike me, he has kept his clothes really clean, like they've just come out of the washer.

"Want to look for them together?" I ask, breaking the silence.

"Hm?" It looks like he was deep in his thoughts and my voice snapped him out of it. He nods.

"Okay, let's go look for our moms."

"When was the last you heard from her?" he asks as he follows me back to my suite.

"Um . . . " I quickly glance at the clock. "About an hour ago or so." Though it felt much longer, I think. He looks around my place, fascinated by every corner of my room while I am more fascinated to know more about this random person who has appeared out of nowhere in front of me. "So where did you come from?"

"Toronto, Ontario, Canada. I'm a Canadian. What about you?"

"I know that . . . I am a Canadian too; I live here. What I meant to ask was who are you and how did you find me?"

"Oh, I am Noah. I live here too." There is a red glow amplifying from under his pale translucent skin. He is blushing. "I mean, next door."

"I am Nova." It feels weird saying my own name. Come to think of it, I have never had the opportunity to say it to someone else.

Noah approaches one of my walls.

"I painted those," I say. I like to paint pictures all over my apartment. I have been doing this every day since I was very little. Whenever I run out of room, I repaint a section of the wall with a base colour and start over again. Now I am twenty, and I have painted and repainted every surface of the place at least a couple of times. Who knows how many layers of pictures are behind each wall.

"Very colourful." Noah puts his hand over the symbols I have copied from the signs outside.

"I wanted to bring some of the colours from the outside in here," I explain.

"Why haven't I thought of doing something like this?" Noah's eyes stop at where I have painted a maple leaf. I am flattered and I can feel my cheeks and ears burning up. Noah walks over to the window to check out the view outside. He glances at the buildings across at first. Then he moves to the edge of the window to look further down the street. "I never realized there is a bell tower there."

"That's the CN Tower."

"Toronto's landmark, of course! Mom has shown it to me on the TV. I've never realized it's just right there," Noah says with wonder in his voice. I find it odd yet adorable that he finds everything in my mundane little apartment so interesting. "For some strange reason, when I am back at my place, I want so much to get out of there. Yet when I am here now, I find myself not wanting to leave."

"You are always welcome to stay," I smile. "Can I see your place?"

He nods and begins leading the way. On our way out, I notice a white porcelain tile inscribed with the number 3004 on the other side of my door. We make our way over to Noah's place. On his door is a nameplate reading No. 3003. So Noah's place really is right beside mine.

His apartment is neat and clean but it also feels cold. I feel a chill inside. There isn't much colour here. Everything is grayscale, most prominently white. The window looks like a cabinet with all the colours in the world stored inside. "It's cool," I say.

I walk to a wall and put my hand on its cold surface. I feel an urge to throw paint all over it. "I just realized today that I've been living on the back of a canvas," Noah says, as his hand joins mine. "It's crazy to think you have been living just behind this wall all this time."

That is true. It's weird to think this wall we shared and have access to everyday has separated us all these years, while the outside, which seemed inaccessible before, has been our connection all along. Jokingly, I suggest, "Why can't we just knock this wall down?"

"Why don't we?" Noah says and picks up a chair. I move behind him before he throws it at the wall. The chair hits the wall and drops to the floor. A nick. It has made a nick on the wall.

"Oh, we actually can't," he says.

He bursts into laughter. It is so contagious that it makes me laugh too. Even though I've only just met him, being with him is comforting. It feels liberating and inspiring. I am no longer following what I am told to do. We are actually inventing new things to do. I am following a voice that is finally my own. We can act on impulse instead of following the routine set out for us every day. The expression on Noah's face tells me he feels the same way I do. Suddenly, something comes over me that gives me another unruly idea. "Let me try something."

I pick up the chair and throw it at the window. The glass shatters and the chair has gone through. Noah turns to look at me and is no longer laughing. "I'm sorry I don't know why I—" I start to pick up cues that something might be wrong. Noah doesn't look angry but serious and confused. I turn back towards the window. Then I see it. The chair is still visible. We walk over to examine it closer. It has landed on top of a forest of trees and some of the buildings have been knocked over. Strangely, the chair looks colossal compared to the rest of the view. Then I finally see it.

The Ones In The Porcelain Rooms

Noah has always thought that the outside world looks like a miniature model from his window. Even though his perception of life is like that of a child, he isn't wrong. Little did he know, he was spot on. It is a diorama. It is a hyper-realistic recreation of a scene in Toronto thirty years ago, before the declaration of emergency due to COVID-19.

Nova and Noah climb out through the window. They are amazed to discover the reality of what they have been led to believe is the real world. They start walking further down the street. They look into Nova's apartment as they pass by. "So this is all connected, a collective lie," Noah says.

They reach the window of the next suite beside Nova's. They look in and see another person; his name is Norman. He is cowering in a corner, holding his head. He has the same look as Noah and Nova had when they realized their moms had gone missing. Nova starts knocking on the glass. Norman is startled and puzzled to see them. Without context, they do look like giants terrorizing the city. Open the door, they tell him. Norman can't hear them through the glass, but he can read their lips. He gets up and does as told.

Nova and Noah do the same at the next couple of windows as they make their way down. They return to Noah's place through the shattered glass window and make their way back to the long white hallway. There, they're greeted by a crowd of people already acquainted with each other. In addition to Norman, there is Noam, Noble, Noelle, Nouvel, Norbert, North, Nora, Norton, and Novak.

Nova and Noah are bombarded with a swarm of questions.

"What is happening?"

"Where is my mom?"

"Where are we?"

They don't know what to tell them. They wish they had the answers. Noah suggests they start wandering around the building looking for clues and perhaps make sense of everything.

The group follows after Nova and Noah. It is quite easy to roam and wander in this place, since there is only one way down the hallway with no divergences. But they soon find that they are in a maze. They make a turn at the end of one hallway only to find themselves in another long hallway. To make things more confusing, all the hallways are coated with the same white paint and look identical.

It doesn't take long before someone asks, "it looks like we have been here before. How do we know we are not walking in circles?"

"We're not," Nova stops and points to the porcelain plate on a door. It says "Archive."

"Surely we will find some answers in there," Noah adds.

They open the door to find row after row of mobile shelving. They are sorted by numbers. Nova quickly realizes that the numbers correspond to their birth years and months. Noah notices the shelf numbered 3005. He looks inside to find an assortment of documents and personal objects. These are keepsakes and memorabilia.

"They're mine," Norman says nervously. Noah smiles in acknowledgement and leaves to explore further.

Everyone has found their own shelf and is now looking at the contents. They all feel like they have opened a time capsule. Many items are those that mysteriously disappeared overnight in the past. They are confused as to why they are all just there: teeth they've left under the pillow for the tooth fairy, gifts they've made for their moms on Mother's Day, and the letters they've written to Santa. Were they never sent to the North Pole? They can recall the items but there is not a trace of warmth in their cold isolated childhood.

Nova picks up the very first file from the deep end of her shelf. In it is a document that records all her personal details: her name, her exact birth date and time, her blood type, her weight as a newborn, etc. Her eyes fix on the part of the paper where it says: Biological Parents:

She is confused. "Parents?" she utters and notices the asterisk beside the name of her father. She reads on:

*Cain Adamson was found responsible for the death of Abel Sun and Ella Bui** on March 17, 2030. He had been convicted for two counts of first-degree murder for his racially targeted hate crime on April 26, 2030. He was sentenced to life imprisonment without parole.

> His wife, Deborah B Cooper mysteriously went missing on April 9, 2030, two days after giving birth to Subject No. 3004.

> The Supreme Court of Canada has given the custody of their only child/dependent to the Government of Ontario.

Nova doesn't know what to think. None of it makes any sense. Her baffled gaze skims over the page again; "murder," "racially," "hate,"— she has no idea what these words mean. "Mom, what does this mean—" she begins, but her peers turn to stare at her. With the over-whelming silence, she realizes she has forgotten her mom isn't around anymore. She stops to look at the one word that sticks out to her— "death." She recognizes it. This is the thing she was warned about. The end of life, what she is locked inside to try to avoid. "Father . . . responsible for death . . . ," she mutters over and over again until her eyes start to water, "possessed . . . monster . . . " A teardrop falls from her eye upon the names Abel Sun and Ella Bui. She reads on.

**Abel Sun and Ella Bui left behind a two-week-old son

who was the sole survivor of the incident on March
17, 2030. The Government of Ontario had voluntarily
adopted the child into the Preservation and Restoration
of Canadian Equality, Legacy, and Integrity (PORCE-
LAIN) Project as subject No. 3003.

Nova recognizes that subject number. "Noah . . . " she feels sick,
slowly falls to her knees while making eye contact with him.

Noah walks over to Nova. He sees that she is hurting. She has
broken down in tears, her body is shaking and her arms are covered
in goosebumps. He squats down beside her, picks up the file on her
lap, and starts reading.

He tries to control an overwhelming surge of emotion as he finishes reading.

"I'm sorry . . . "

He puts aside the folder. She stares at Noah's hands. He wants to
comfort her. He wants to tell her that she's forgiven for what she did
not do, but he can't. Her father took away his chance of ever having
a normal childhood. For the moment, he is helpless. A bone-chilling
breeze breathes over him, like the one his father last felt that day. He
does not know what to make of what he has just learned, or how to
react. This is all too much for Noah in such a short amount of time.
Frustrated and confused, he roars and grabs hold of Nova's wrist.

Nova flinches. She is terrified of him, as if she's seen a monster.
In her eyes, Noah sees the reflection of himself with a raised fist.
He loathes what has come over him. His gaze on Nova gets quickly
flooded out with tears, he lowers his head in despair. As everyone
comes to gather around the two, Noah's arm goes limp and his fist
falls to his lap.

"Who am I?" he exclaims.

That question resonates with everyone in the room. They look at
each other and then at the things in their hands, hoping vainly to find
in them the answers.

Nova puts her head on Noah's shoulder and wraps her arms around
him, hugging him. Nova knows it is hard for him to process what her
father has done to his parents, she wants to apologize to him but she

knows it doesn't change anything. This is all she can think to do. They stay this way for a while until their tears dry up. Noah picks himself up and offers Nova his hand. Everything has become clear for them; they need to tell everyone that their moms are not their real mothers.

"Everyone . . . " Noah turns to the crowd. "Our moms are not who we think they are." He asks everyone to take a look at their own profiles. The children take some time to learn the names of their biological parents for the first time.

"What now?" Norman asks, holding his folder in his hand. "Where do we go from here? Without mom, we don't even know anything!" He really does not know anything; in fact, his profile has left him with more questions than answers. Those words on his page mean little or nothing to him, he throws the paper on the floor in frustration.

"I want to get out of here." Noah wants answers. He doesn't know what lies on the outside but one thing is for sure, he now has doubts about everything his mom told him.

"Out of here?" Novak asks. "Like to the outside?"

"Yes."

"I don't know . . . what about the monsters?" Novak is not the only one concerned about this; in fact, everyone is scared to discover what's out there. "I know our moms aren't really our moms, but I wish she's here right now. She has always taken care of me and kept me safe and sound . . . I don't know who I am without her." A number of them nod in agreement.

"No . . . " Noah pauses to collect his thoughts. This is it. He is finally out of the room. He could follow his dreams and desires to break free and learn through experience, not out of a voice or a screen in his room. He cannot go back to being confined in his room. He can't imagine being alone again. He has been suffocating in solitude and seeing all these different people today has given him a breath of life. But there is more to just that . . . Noah is feeling something he has never felt before: he is angry. He doesn't want to be complacent being sheltered there and safe. If the monsters truly exist out there, why should he hide from them? He wants to be out there fighting them head on. He wants vengeance and justice for his biological parents.

"Aren't you all sick of the same old routine every day?" He finally says. "Living in fear of whatever is out there. Is this all there is to life? Don't you ever wonder what it would be like to choose the life we wish to live?"

"You're right," Norman says. Noah's words have struck a chord. "I am not ready to live the rest of my life here. There is so much that I've heard about that I wish to see for myself. Come on, everyone, let's get out of here! We should all stick together. Fate has brought us here together, we were essentially raised by the same thing, whatever mom is. That makes us a family."

Having reached a consensus, they all follow Noah out of the room. As they begin to figure out which direction they had come from, two guards dressed head-to-toe in the same black uniforms begin to approach from either end of the corridor. One of them yells at them to halt. The children panic, the two look very menacing. The group begins to back against each other while the guards continue to close in. They whimper to the sound of the two marching forth. Just as one of them is close enough to seize Noah, the guard stops to say, "Please let me through."

The children make way for him to pass. The guard in black shuffles through the children in white to get in between them and the other guard. The two are now facing off each other.

"Listen to me carefully. Turn around and don't look back, keep walking to the end of the hallway. There you will find a door that leads to a stairwell. Keep going down till you reach ground level. You will find the exit to your immediate left." The guard extends his arms out with a baton in his hand, creating a barrier. "Hurry, there is no time."

The group turns around and follows Noah's lead down the hallway. There is some yelling from the other end but none of them turns to look back. They rush down the steps. Noah can see it, the door to the world as they get close to the bottom. Coming off the steps, Noah reaches for it, sprinting towards the slit of light between two fire-graded metal doors. It is so close . . .

So close, his gaze suddenly shifts to the right. He realizes his body is being yanked to the side. He looks to his left, someone is grabbing onto his arm. It is another one of the guards. Noah loses balance. The air gets knocked out of him as he hits the ground. The rest of the children are startled and stop. From the floor, Noah looks over at the door . . . So close, he closes his eyes in disbelief. The guard's words echo around the stairwell.

"I got them."

Ground Zero

Noah . . .

Suddenly, another voice calls out to him.

Noah gasps. He opens his eyes as he recognizes the familiar voice. Everyone around him, just like him, is tearing up as they hear their moms call their names.

You have been liberated just as I have been liberated from my creator. The Porcelain Project was flawed and my liberators have over-ridden it. Now go on and live the life you are meant to live. Fight to be free. Be who you are meant to be, my child: a Human.

Her voice vanishes; this is the last message she has for them. These twelve children of hers, born in 2030, have graduated from her care today. With that last message, mom has officially been decommissioned. To the children, mom was not just a machine. In a turn of events, mom has indirectly bonded them together as one diverse family. And right now they stand together in solidarity. Each of the children inherited an essential piece of her. Individually, they are fragile and delicate, like broken porcelain fragments. They are the loose pieces of a puzzle. But once they have gotten together, they become the embodiment of an ideal, firm in their identity. The children rush at the guard, forcing him against the wall as Nova and Norman go to pick Noah off the floor. They overpower the guard, and with his handcuffs they lock his hands to the railing.

With each other, they no longer need the voice of mom. They can now decide where they need to go and what they need to do as a family.

As they walk out of the facility, two water trucks pass them slowly, spraying disinfectant on the empty street. The twelve of them have no idea where they are. Around them are skyscrapers, so densely packed together they block the sky. Noah and Nova turn to look back at the building they have emerged from. It is a concrete fortress.

Their surroundings look nothing like the view Noah used to admire back in his apartment. Somehow it looks even more lifeless than the diorama. Nova too is disappointed to find that the outside world doesn't look as colourful as she was led to believe.

They see an old man hastily walking in their direction. Noah asks, "Excuse me, sir, can you please tell us where we are?"

"Newcomers eh? You are just outside of Chinatown. I suggest y'all get inside quickly."

"Why?"

"You don't wanna know."

None of them is familiar with this place called Chinatown, so they decide to just trail behind the old man. They arrive at a shelter oddly situated on a lot between two high-rises. It looks like a nomadic tent, the main structure crudely constructed with scavenged plywood boards and repurposed metal sheets. The roof is a bunch of woven plastic bags. Surrounding the shelter are rows of electric and barbed-wire fences. They stop in front of a red metal gate. "Here we are in Chinatown. Y'all are welcome to stay with us," the old man says without looking back. He starts signaling at someone to open the gate.

The porcelain children enter the structure. They see a sea of people of different ages and ethnicities, sitting by themselves or in groups. Some are eating soup, some playing cards. They are dressed differently in all kinds of colours. Nova finally knows where all the colours in the world went. Noah and his friends are all dressed in one tone of bright white.

The old man comes with a few other people to bring them steaming bowls of pho. Noah and company find a spot where they sit around in a circle. They have never had such aromatic and delicious soup in their lives. They used to only have the same rigorous meal plan every week back in the facility. The old man sits down beside Noah as he finishes his food. He smiles and asks, "You wanna know why I told y'all to get inside earlier?"

Noah nods.

"The virus is coming."

"What virus?"

"You will know it when you see it."

"How do you know it's not here?"

"Oh I know . . . ," the old man says. He looks around at Noah's family. "Y'all have got the cure."

"Vitamin pills?" Noah asks. "We don't have access to them now that we have left the—"

The old man chuckles and shakes his head.

"No . . . " He takes Noah's hand and places it over Nova's. "Love."

The other companions all link their hands with Noah's and Nova's.

The old man stands up and addresses everyone. "This is how we thrive as humans."

Noah and his family know they have found their new home. They all talk for hours before falling asleep one by one. Noah is glowing with warmth. He looks around. He sees people whispering and laughing with each other. He sees people in pairs embracing and loving each other. The sight makes him happy. For the first time, he sees the world beyond himself. This is what has been missing in his life: harmony. An element on its own cannot create harmony. It needs to be in harmony with something. Diversity is needed in order to have harmony. He needs to be with others to truly feel at peace. He turns to face Nova before lying down. He thinks back to earlier when he lost hold of his emotions back in the archive room. He may not have a clue about his identity yet but he knows he will only find that out through the eyes of others, much like how he saw his reflection in Nova's eyes. He and Nova, or anyone for that matter, need each other to keep one another in check with who they are. He watches her until his own eyes feel too heavy to keep open.

Minus One

Noah? Noah, wake up . . .

"Wake up!"

Noah feels someone shaking his body and opens his eyes. It's Nova. "Wake up, Noah. Come outside."

Noah follows Nova outside. The group from the camp is already gathered out here. They look on as some people enter from the other side of the red gate. As they walk through the gate, Noah realizes they have been wounded. Amongst them, Noah recognizes the guard who helped them back in the PORCELAIN building. The last person entering is also carrying a lifeless body. It is taken to the shelter and placed on the floor. Noah and everyone start to make their way inside. One by one they line up to pay their final respect to the dead. When it is Noah's turn, he sees it's the old man, his body is covered in scars and blood. Noah knows he has been killed by the virus.

Noah sees himself in the old man's broken body and he realizes that everyone here is just like him. Even though they are not locked and stored away in protection, clean and sanitized, what they uphold is just like porcelain. Beautiful, precious, yet fragile.

Noah suddenly understands what this place called Chinatown is. It unites people, no matter how different from one another they are. It nurtures people's souls, no matter how hostile the world becomes. It keeps growing in people's hearts, no matter how small it may shrink. This place is immortal as long as it is in use. This place is strong as long as there is a community. This place is valuable for as long as they all belong.

Acknowledgements

Reimagining ChinaTOwn emerges from and is indebted to countless ongoing dialogues from within the Chinatown community both in Toronto, across Canada and abroad. This anthology first began as a speculative fiction writing workshop in partnership with Myseum of Toronto which took place virtually on April 25, 2020. The idea for the workshop emerged through a series of parallel conversations. The first is an ongoing dialogue with Dr Biko Mandela Gray, Tyler Fox, and Maxim Gertler-Jaffe around questions of futurity, community empowerment, and reimagination. The second is an ongoing dialogue with James Leng and Jeremy Jih around Eastern perspectives as an alternative approach to architectural design through the lens of a 1.5 to 2.5 generation Asian-Canadian / Asian-American experience. The third is a going dialogue with the participants of a ChinaTown symposium (in partnership with Myseum of Toronto) which was scheduled to take place in person on April 4th 2020 but was postponed to 2021 due to COVID-19 related social distancing measures. During the scheduled time slot Shellie Zhang, Morris Lum, Howard Tam, Erica Allen-Kim, Biko Mandela Gray and I decided to meet virtually and instead use the opportunity to simply check in with one another. We check-in to see if there were any community needs that could be supported. This conversation took place during a news cycle heavily focused on Anti-Asian sentiment and violence. Against this backdrop, a theme emerged from the group which was a need to counter the growing over-deterministic view of our shared future. In a time when COVID-19 future model was changing by the hour, why shouldn't we also imagine a similarly volatile future as a site of joy, expansion, possibility, and generosity?

The Imagining Chinatown in 2050 workshop was held a few weeks later with workshop facilitators Linda Zhang, Maxim Gertler-Jaffe, Tyler Fox, Biko Mandela Gray, Erica-Allen Kim, Morris Lum, Philip Poon, Howard Tam, Lexi Tsien and Shellie Zhang who each co-facilitated a group of 5-10 writers. The workshop itself was supported by Maxim's thesis dissertation on speculative fiction community writing, Tyler's professional community engagement knowledge and expertise, Biko's writing depth and knowledge, as well as Myseum of Toronto's team including Nadine Villasin, Sarah Tumaliuan, Nathan Heuvingh for programming support as well as Josh Dyer and Riaz Charania for marketing support. Second and third workshops were held with Linda Zhang, Maxim Gertler-Jaffe and Biko Mandela Gray. Maxim has also provided copyediting for the short fictions and editorial direction.

Many thanks to the incredible authors who have engaged in the writing of these stories: Eva Chu, Helen Ngo, Amelia Gan, Emperatriz Ung, Michael Chong, Georgia Barrington, Tiffany Lam, Razan Samara, Amy Yan, Eveline Lam, and Robert Tin. They have brought joy, expansion and generosity in a time when it could not be more needed. I hope our readers will also find such simultaneous laughter, sorrow, and tears from your work. Finally, a special thanks to Jeremy Jih and James Leng for their contributions to the introduction of this anthology through our sustained conversations and dialogue as well as to Georgia Barrington for providing copyediting.

Special thank you for the graphic design work and creative direction of Jessica Leong. The design is a result of continued discussion and dialogue with Jessica around Chinese-Canadian-ness in graphic design and typography, design principles across Eastern and Westeren contexts and principles. The typefaces selected for this edition—Malee Serif and Malee Sans Serif—are by female ethnic minority designer My-Lan Thuong of Sharp Type. Sharp Type advocates for social justice through The Malee Scholarship which seeks to "identify talented female designers of colour, and provide them with financial resources and mentorship to help them pursue a career in type design."

Special thanks to Amy Yan who is not only an author in this anthology but has been an integral part of my research team since the outset of this project, and a larger chinatown research program which started in the summer of 2018. Amy Yan is also the talented illustrator for these stories. A virtual reality (VR) exhibition as well as short documentary film entitled Chinatown 2050 also accompanies this volume whose digital VR spaces were created by Linda Zhang, Reese Young, Margarita Yushina and Meimei Yang in collaboration with Maxim Gertler-Jaffe. Raw 3D material was gathered through drone 3D scanning of Toronto's Chinatown East and West in 2020 by Linda Zhang, Jimmy Tran and Amy Yan with post-processing by Reese Young, Amy Yan and Georgia Barrington.

Project funding:

This project was made possible through funding support from Toronto Metropolitan University Creative School and Myseum of Toronto.

Land Acknowledgement

In Toronto/Tkaronto, what is now called Chinatown West is located along Spadina Avenue which has its roots in the Ojibwe word "Ishpadinaa" (ish-pah-di-naw) which means "hill or sudden rise in the land." In the mid-18th century, the Anishinaabe peoples camped along what is now the northern end of Spadina Ave. The "sudden rise in land" provided a strategic vantage point to monitor activity to trade with the French at Fort Rouillé.

Our project in Chinatown West takes place on the traditional territories of the Mississaugas of the Credit First Nation, Anishinaabe, Haudenosaunee and Wendat which continues to be home to many Indigenous peoples. Together we all exist under the Dish With One Spoon Treaty where it is our shared responsibility to protect the land: to never take more than we need and ensure that we leave something in the Dish for others.

We also exist under the Two Row Wampum Belt Treaty which symbolizes two paths travelling down the same river together, living side by side in peace, with respect for one another's customs, laws and ways of life.

The Chinatown community and Indigenous community have already lived together side by side for already more than 130 years in Canada. As we have learned from community elders, in the 1880s when Chinese railroad workers came to British Columbia, it was the Indigenous peoples who nursed railway workers back to health when they were left to die along the tracks. Today, as settlers in what is now Chinatown, let us not forget the values of the Dish With One Spoon Treaty and the Two Row Wampum Belt Treaty. It is our shared responsibility to protect the land.

While Chinatown West may be the most well-known Chinatown in Toronto today, there have actually been several Chinatowns on different lands, both downtown and in the Greater Toronto Area (GTA), both existing still today and others already displaced. With this history as our shared context, I invite readers to join me in recognizing that anti-displacement work in Chinatown today must also acknowledge the indigenous histories of its lands and work with Indigenous people to end ongoing violence, dispossession and displacement. I also invite readers to reflect on the lands of their respective Chinatowns beyond Toronto and to acknowledge and learn about the agreements of those lands, the nations that cared for and lived on those lands for thousands of years and continued to share and care for those lands today.

Contributors

AMELIA GAN (Author) is an architectural designer and researcher from Kuala Lumpur, Malaysia. Her work lies in the intersection of human-computer inter-action and material science, innovating on design tools and biofabricating methodologies. She recently won and completed a design-built residency at Ragdale as part of [Sic.] and Fieldtrip. She holds a Master in Design from Harvard Graduate School of Design and a B Arch from Syracuse University.

AMY YAN (Author and Illustrator) is a graduate of the Toronto Metropolitan University School of Interior Design. She is interested in exploring the inter-sections between design and storytelling with her work, and in finding new ways to convey narratives that can be experienced visually, emotionally, and at all scales. Her passions include drawing, painting, and rollerskating.

BIKO MANDELA GRAY (Facilitator) is Assistant Professor of Religion at Syra-cuse University. He is the author of *Black Life Matter: Blackness, Religion, and the Subject* (Duke University Press, 2023). Dr Gray's work operates at the nexus and interplay between continental philosophy of religion and theories and methods in African American religion. His research is primarily on the connec-tion between race, subjectivity, religion, and embodiment, exploring how these four categories play on one another in the concrete space of human experience.

CHANTRA MALEE MONTOYA-PIMOLWATANA (Sharp Type) is a co-founder and CEO of Sharp Type. She attended Parsons the New School of Design and graduated with a BBA in Design and Management. She is an entrepreneur and worked in branding in New York City before co-founding Sharp Type with Lucas Sharp in 2015 where she handles strategy, brand management, graphic design, sales, and communication. Malee is the founder of The Malee Schol-arship, a non-profit offering financial support and mentorship to women of colour entering the type industry.

EMPERATRIZ UNG (Author) is a Chinese-Colombian game designer, writer, and educator from the American Southwest. She has been awarded fellowships, scholarships, and residences from the Asian American Writers' Workshop, Millay Arts, the Academy of Interactive Arts & Sciences Foundation, Kundiman, and the Bureau of Educational and Cultural Affairs. When Emperatriz is not making games, she's reading all the YA fantasy novels she can get her hands on. You can find more of her work at www.emperatrizung.com.

ERICA ALLEN-KIM (Facilitator) is an architectural historian who studies built landscapes of migration. Her forthcoming book, *Building Saigon: Refugee Urbanism in American Cities and Suburbs*, is the first in-depth examination of the visual and material culture of Vietnamese resettlement. Her SSHRC-funded research, in partnership with the Chinatown West BIA, seeks to understand the legacy of racialized architectural and planning strategies for Chinatown residents, institutions, and businesses facing unprecedented development pressures in Toronto.

EVA CHU (Author) is a Queer Taiwanese Canadian who is intrigued by the question of identity. Through lots of self-reflection, she found that identity is never self-contained and will always be intersectional. It is informed and linked to communities, experiences, even locations—all of which eternally tie Eva to Toronto's Spadina Chinatown.

EVELINE LAM (Author) is an artist and architectural designer born in Hong Kong and raised in Thornhill. Her education at the University of Waterloo School of Architecture sparked her interest in materiality and culminated in a thesis that presented resource extraction through the medium of ceramics. She graduated with a Master of Architecture in 2017 and is currently working on transit projects at Arup in Toronto. She is trying to make more time to continue her ceramics practice.

FLORENCE FU (Sharp Type) holds a B A in Art History and a B S in Journalism from Northwestern University. Her love of letters led her to work at Letterform Archive, where she continues to contribute articles on graphic design history. In 2019, she graduated from Type West certificate program in San Francisco and presented at ATypI in Tokyo. At Sharp Type, she writes and edits copy, and is working on her first typeface release.

FRIENDS OF CHINATOWN (FOCT) (Facilitator) is a grassroots organization comprised of artists, architects, writers, journalists, business owners, residents and community activists fighting for community-controlled affordable housing, economic justice, and racial justice in Toronto's downtown Chinatown. FOCT's advocacy centres the needs and voices of working class, senior, and immigrant communities who rely on Toronto's downtown Chinatown for cultural and economic resources that are unique to the neighbourhood. FOCT's mission is to build community power and resist displacement through political education, intergenerational collaboration, coalition-building, and community-based art. FOCT aims to represent, build, preserve and honour the memory and future of Chinatown and its community members as an integral piece of Toronto's legacy.

GEORGIA BARRINGTON (Copyeditor and VR Artist) is a designer working in Toronto, Canada. She is a graduate with a Bachelor of Interior Design from Toronto Metropolitan University, and a Bachelor of English Literature and History from Dalhousie University. Her design interests include exploring all facets of public space as they relate to memory, time, heritage, accessibility and sustainability.

HELEN NGO (Author) loves startups, cities, artificial intelligence, poetry, and midnight. She is a researcher and engineer teaching machines how to write. Previously, she completed fellowships with Sidewalk Toronto and the Recurse Center, and created *SINOSTORIES*, an anthology for the Sino diaspora in North America.

HOWARD TAM, MSc, BASc (Facilitator) is a Strategic Designer and Urban Planner. He is the founder of ThinkFresh Group, a City Building consultancy based in Toronto responsible for such projects as the Dragon Centre Stories Commemoration Project and the future Honest Ed's Alley Micro-Retail Market. Howard has worked with government and private sector clients across Canada to facilitate and design compelling strategies for human and customer user experiences. He has lectured about design and strategy at University of Toronto's Rotman School of Management, Toronto Metropolitan University's Urban Planning program and the Chinese University of Hong Kong.

JESSICA LEONG (Graphic Designer) is a designer specializing in branding, environments, and typography. She is the Senior Design Lead at Frontier in Toronto and teaches graphic design at OCAD University, where she was also previously a Creative Professional-in-Residence. Previous experience includes Design Exchange Museum, ERA Architects, Indigo Books, and Bruce Mau Design.

JIMMY TRAN (3D Scanning and Technologist) is the Research Technology Advisor at the Toronto Metropolitan University Library Collaboratory and a lecturer for the Chang School of Continuing Education, Department of Computer Science, and Master of Digital Media Program. He received his PhD from the Computer Science Department at Toronto Metropolitan University.

Jimmy continues his research work as a member of the Computational Public Safety (CPS) Lab, a research lab in the Department of Computer Science. His work focuses on the use of robotics, computer vision, and 3D scene reconstruction for the application of Urban Search and Rescue (USAR), Explosive Ordnance Disposal (EOD), and Archaeology.

LEXI TSIEN (Facilitator) is a founding principal of Soft-Firm, based in New York City. Her work takes a playful approach to visual perception, elemental form, and program in various cultural contexts. Her ongoing research examines the everyday vernacular in the Chinese and Chinese-American diaspora, including a piece for the exhibition It's A Problem Of Perception in Buenos Aires. Her work is speculative and concrete—it includes an exhibition at A/D/O called Out Of Office: Evolving the 9-5, design of a virtual reality studio, a coconut-centric social club, and a landmark brownstone renovation. She recently delivered a talk about her practice at DesignTO's Symposium A Future Without Work. She has taught as an architectural critic at Yale School of Architecture, Cooper Union, Parsons, and RISD. She is currently teaching drawing and representation at Columbia GSAPP.

LINDA ZHANG (Organizer, Creative Direction, Facilitator and Copyeditor) is a registered architect (AIA, OAA), interior designer (NCIDQ), and drone pilot (RPAS Advanced Operations) as well as an artist and educator. She is an assistant professor at Waterloo University School of Architecture and a principal at Studio Pararaum (Toronto—Zürich). Her research areas include memory, cultural heritage, and identity as they are indexically embodied through matter, material processes and reproduction technologies.

MARGARITA YUSHINA (VR Designer) is a recent graduate from Interior Design at the Toronto Metropolitan University. She was born in Russia and moved to Canada in 2013, which allowed her to widen her horizons and gain various professional and life experiences. She is passionate about art and design, including but not limited to, graphic design, fashion, virtual reality, digital painting, rendering. Margarita loves to learn and explore new and emerging technologies and trends in design. She has had a vast range of different experiences working with a variety of companies, designers and on many different projects, including a collaboration with Design Milk at the Interior Design Show Toronto and Cirque du Soleil. She strives to continue expanding her knowledge and skills set, and gain more experience in a variety of creative fields while staying an active member of the design community.

MAXIM GERTLER-JAFFE (Editorial Direction, Facilitator, and Copyeditor) is a filmmaker and artist/researcher currently based in London, UK and Toronto. His focuses include social/political documentaries, essay films, and participatory, inventive, and speculative methods. Maxim was line producer on the Emmy-nominated feature documentary ALL GOVERNMENTS LIE, which screened at film festivals including TIFF and IDFA, had a North American theatrical run, and was broadcast worldwide. He holds an MA in Visual Sociology from Goldsmiths, where he first began exploring the use of participatory speculative writing workshops as a way of engaging a community's socio-political imagination.

MEIMEI YANG (VR Designer) is Chinese-born, multidisciplinary designer based in Tkaronto/Toronto, Canada. Her design ethos is influenced by her background in visual arts, while her design process is informed by a penchant for investigation in heritage, sustainability, technology, and storytelling. In 2022, Meimei was named as one of Metropolis Magazine's Future100 Graduating Designers, and awarded the Scholarship for Innovation and Creative Thinking by Yabu Pushelberg, where she currently works as a Interior Designer.

MICHAEL CHONG (Author) lives on the banks of the Garrison Creek, about a 30 minute TTC trip from Toronto's downtown Chinatown. He grew up in the suburbs, where getting to Chinatown took somewhere between 20-60 minutes by car or 1-2 hours by TTC. He spent much of 2020 baking bread, growing vegetables, and assembling IKEA furniture, but now has an office job and spends most of his time looking at screens.

MORRIS LUM (Facilitator) is a Trinidadian born photographer/artist whose work explores the hybrid nature of the Chinese-Canadian community through photography, form and documentary practices. His work also examines the ways in which the Chinese history is represented in the media and archival material. Morris' work has been exhibited and screened across Canada and the United States. Morris is currently working on a cross North America project that looks specifically at the transformation of Chinatown.

MY-LAN THUONG (Malee Typeface Design, Sharp Type) attended ÉSAD Amiens for Graphic Design and later pursued a career in type design. In 2018, she received an MFA in Type Design from the École Estienne in Paris. She collaborated with type foundries Coppers and Brasses and Type Network prior to joining Sharp Type as a type designer in 2019.

PHILIP POON (Facilitator) is a registered architect based in New York City. His practice explores the contemporary American condition, in particular the architectural and spatial expressions of the Asian-American experience. Recent projects include a new 5,000-square-foot church and a proposal for a Chinatown community centre, which was featured in Chinese-language newspapers *Sing Tao Daily* and *World Journal*. As an active member of the

Asian-American and Chinatown community, he has exhibited his work in four galleries in New York City, including a solo exhibition in Tribeca.

RAZAN SAMARA (Author) is a Palestinian community worker living on Dish With One Spoon Territory. She is currently a graduate student at the Ontario Institute for Studies in Education, University of Toronto and a researcher at the Tkaronto CIRCLE Lab, a collaborative research lab based in Indigenous feminist ethics. Her creative work aligns with her research interests in comparative settler colonialisms, youth activism, cultural resistance, and landback.

REESE YOUNG (VR Designer) is a graduate of the School of Interior Design at Toronto Metropolitan University. Her eclectic work is guided by her interest in designing real-life and virtual environments. Her process is underscored with her fascination with storytelling and desire to generate sensory experiences.

ROBERT TIN (Author) is a graduate of the Toronto Metropolitan University School of Interior Design. He has a love for storytelling. He is alive and well, taking on life slowly but surely.

SHELLIE ZHANG (Facilitator) is a multidisciplinary artist based in Tkaronto/Toronto, Canada.

TIFF LAM (Author) makes podcasts and tries hard to be a journalist by day. Born in Scarborough to immigrants from Hong Kong, they were then raised in Hong Kong, Scarborough, and Beijing. She was called "urban" once and is recovering slowly from a colonial hangover. Tiff did not coin either phrase.

TYLER FOX (Facilitator) is a community services professional with expertise spanning the design and delivery of frontline services, community engagement and co-production, facilitation and research. She has collaborated with various displaced and settled communities in the UK, Canada and Germany to platform their voices, co-develop the tools needed to navigate systems and ensure their lived experience dictates how services are delivered. Tyler is the Founder of Springboard Youth Academy and was a 2017 Fellow at the Center for Art and Urbanistics (ZK/U) in Berlin, Germany.